Something horrible had happened in the wilderness.

Danielle ran to Jack before he'd reached the end of the trail. "Tell me what you found."

The dim light accented the sadness in his eyes. "We found Tricia's body."

"W-w-was it like the Web site?"

He took her arm and guided her across the parking lot. Then he slumped against the side of the car and rubbed his hands over his eyes. "It was horrible."

Danielle's concern for Jack overshadowed her grief for Tricia. Nothing she could do would help the young woman, but Jack needed someone to care about him.

She stared up into his face. "I know what you're feeling. I've been there."

The hard lines of his face softened. "I still can't believe what some people are capable of doing."

"You're a man who doesn't share his feelings, but that doesn't mean you don't have any. I can tell you're strong, and you'll be able to do your job."

He straightened. "Thanks. I'm glad I brought you with me tonight."

Books by Sandra Robbins

Love Inspired Suspense

Final Warning
Mountain Peril

SANDRA ROBBINS,

a native West Tennessean, is a former teacher and principal in the Tennessee public schools. She now writes full-time and is an adjunct college professor. She is married and has four children and five grandchildren.

Her fascination with mystery and suspense can be traced to all the Nancy Drew books she read as a child. She hopes her stories will entice readers to keep turning the pages until wrongs have been righted and romance has blossomed in her characters' lives.

It is her prayer that God will use her words to plant seeds of hope in the lives of her readers. Her greatest desire is that many will come to know the peace she draws from her life verse *Isaiah* 40:31—*But those who hope in the Lord will renew their strength. They will soar on wings like eagles, they will run and not grow weary, they will walk and not be faint.*

To find out more about Sandra and her books, go to her Web site at www.sandrarobbins.net.

SANDRA ROBBINS

MOUNTAIN PERIL

Steeple Hill®

Published by Steeple Hill Books™

STEEPLE HILL BOOKS

Steeple
Hill®

Recycling programs
for this product may
not exist in your area.

ISBN-13: 978-0-373-67412-1

MOUNTAIN PERIL

You are forgiving and good, O Lord,
abounding in love to all who call to you.
—*Psalms* 86:5

To my dear husband who has encouraged me in my writing journey. Without his love and support this book wouldn't have been possible.

ONE

The Webster Falls Sheriff's Department Asks for Help in Apprehending a Killer.

The flashing words, accompanied by the steady drone of a drumbeat and the eerie sound of distant guitars, hovered above a picture that sent chills down Danielle Tyler's back. She leaned closer to the computer screen and stared spellbound at the scene below the words. As Dean of Students at Webster University, she was familiar with some of the Web sites her students frequented, but she'd never seen anything like this.

A young girl lay on her back, her dark hair fanned out on a pillow of mountain foliage underneath. Red-tinged leaves littered her blood-drenched clothes. Her open eyes stared upward as if offering a silent plea for release from pain.

Danielle closed her eyes for a moment to shut out

the grisly scene of the girl she knew so well and reopened them to stare at Detective Jack Denton from the Webster Falls Sheriff's Department sitting across from her desk. "H-how did you find this horrible site?"

He opened the notebook he held and glanced at a page. "A man named Harrison Coleman from Marietta, Georgia, called our department this morning. He said his son who attends Georgia Tech said the Web site has become the main topic of conversation on the campus. When I pulled it up, I was surprised at what I saw."

Danielle crossed her arms and hugged herself to suppress the icy feeling flowing through her body. "It's given me quite a shock, too."

"I can understand. I intended to take this to the university's president, but when I arrived, his secretary told me he was in Asheville today. She suggested I bring it to you."

Danielle nodded. "Dr. Newman will be back tomorrow. In the meantime, how can I help you?"

The muscle in the detective's jaw twitched. "The Web site claims the girl on there is a Webster student and has been murdered." He paused before he continued. "Our department doesn't know anything about a murder, but we're concerned that the scene is identical to the murder ten years ago of Jennifer McCaslin who was a student here."

Danielle took a deep breath. "I realized that when I saw the picture."

A frown creased his forehead. "Did you know Jennifer McCaslin?"

Danielle sank back in her chair. "We were roommates. She was murdered our senior year at Webster." She pointed to the screen. "But this girl's not Jennifer."

"No, I realized that. I looked at a picture from Jennifer McCaslin's cold case file. We don't know who the girl on the Web site is."

Danielle gritted her teeth. "She's Tricia Peterson, a student here at Webster. But I saw her on campus this morning and she was fine. She was only a child when Jennifer was killed. How would she even know about the murder?"

"I don't know."

Danielle glanced back at the screen. "This doesn't make any sense."

"We know that, but we wanted to see if anyone can give us information. From what my caller told me this morning, this Web site is causing panic on college campuses. Not to mention the fact that it doesn't look good that a sheriff's office is advertising for help in catching a killer."

Danielle frowned. "But why are students frightened by this obvious prank?"

He nodded toward the computer. "Why don't you read what it says next?"

Danielle turned back to the computer and read the lines printed underneath the flashing heading.

The Webster Falls, North Carolina, Sheriff's Department asks for your help in the apprehension of Damien Carter, the chief suspect in the murder of Lila Barrett. The victim, a student at Webster University, was found on a Smoky Mountain trail outside of Webster Falls in September. Carter, also a student at the school, disappeared soon after the discovery of the body. Various sightings of the fugitive have been reported, but so far he has eluded capture.

Danielle shook her head and frowned. "We don't have a Lila Barrett or a Damien Carter enrolled at Webster."

Detective Denton nodded. "I know. When I went to the president's office, his secretary told me."

Acquaintances of the suspect report the young man had become obsessed with murders on college campuses and had often threatened to wage his own rampage across the country. Having been blackballed by a fraternity, he harbors animosity against anyone belonging to a Greek organization. Students enrolled in institutions of higher learning are warned to be on the lookout for this suspected killer. If he is seen, notify the Webster Falls, North Carolina, Sheriff's Department at once.

Danielle leaned back in her chair and pointed to the screen. "I can't believe this. Who would construct such a Web site?"

Detective Denton glanced down at the notebook. "Actually we know. Our tech guys traced the Internet Service Provider and found out the Web site owner is Flynn Carter."

Danielle sprang from her chair. "Flynn?" she screeched. "He's my work study student and Tricia's boyfriend. Why would he do this?"

"That's what I need to find out. Can you get Carter in here?"

She reached for the phone, but her hands shook so that it slipped from her fingers. Clutching it with both hands, she brought it to her ear. "Betty, would you find out what class Flynn Carter is in and get him to my office right away?" After hanging up, she glanced at the detective. "Is there anything else?"

Detective Denton nodded. "There are pages of forensics information, a picture of the victim and killer together before the murder. There's even a page with pictures of the suspected killer at places all across the country—Las Vegas, the Grand Canyon, a museum in Oklahoma City, Graceland. It says these photos were sent to the department by tourists who just happened to catch him in their family vacation pictures."

Danielle clicked on the page with the photographs and gasped. "That's Flynn in those pictures."

"That's what I suspected," Detective Denton said.

She started to speak, but Flynn shuffled into the room. Wearing faded jeans with blown-out holes and a muscle-fitted, sueded cotton shirt, he looked like any other Webster student, not the designer of a gruesome Web site. His bleached hair tumbled over his forehead, and he glanced from one to the other, before he settled a deadpan expression on Danielle. "You sent for me, Dr. Tyler?"

She nodded in Detective Denton's direction. "This is Detective Jack Denton, an investigator with the sheriff's office. He'd like to ask you some questions."

A crimson flush spread across his face and forehead. "What about?"

Danielle sucked in her breath and frowned. She opened her mouth, but Detective Denton interrupted her. "I'm here investigating a complaint I had today and need to ask you a few questions."

Flynn tensed. "Fire away."

"Are you responsible for the Web site that claims to document the murder of a Webster student?"

Flynn's body relaxed, and a smirk crossed his face. "Yeah."

The detective's mouth thinned into a straight line.

"Can you explain what made you construct such a site?"

Flynn chuckled. "What's the big deal? It was just a joke. You know, shake some fraternity and sorority kids up a little."

Anger flashed on Jack Denton's face, and he advanced on Flynn. "I don't consider it a joke when our department gets calls from parents in other parts of the country who have kids scared to venture out on their college campuses."

Flynn glanced at Danielle. "You mean they thought it was real?"

The frown on Detective Denton's forehead deepened. "Yeah. There's no telling what harm your little prank has caused. With all the crazy people out there, all it would take would be for one to see your site and decide to copy the murder."

"You've got to be kidding. Nobody would do that."

Detective Denton jabbed his finger at Flynn's chest. "Look, Mr. Smart Guy, if you could see all the information that comes across my desk about copycat crimes, you'd have thought twice before you put up that Web site."

Flynn gritted his teeth. "I can't help it if there are crazy people out there. It has nothing to do with me or my Web site."

"Well, just to make sure, our department wants you to take it down."

Flynn shook his head. "You can't make me do that. My dad's a lawyer, and he's taught me all about my rights. I haven't broken any laws, and you know it."

"That remains to be seen."

Flynn started to respond, but Danielle interrupted him. "I suggest you do as the detective tells you, Flynn, before your enrollment at this university is affected."

Flynn's eyes widened. "Dr. Newman wouldn't kick me out, would he?"

Danielle nodded. "You involved the university when you depicted the murder scene of a former student. Since that case has never been solved, you used information from an ongoing investigation." She paused and took a breath. "And I might add that in all the time I've known you, I've never seen you act as disrespectful as you have today. Now unless the detective has more questions, I want you to leave."

Detective Denton held up his hand. "I do have one more question. What about the pictures on the Web site of you at different spots across the country? How did you pull that off?"

Flynn pulled his attention away from Danielle and faced the detective. "That was really cool, wasn't it?" A laugh rumbled in his throat. "A friend and I drove from California when we came back to school. We stopped at tourist attractions along the way. We'd spot a family group. I'd walk over close to them, and my friend would snap the picture. I posted them and said they were pictures sent from people who caught a killer by mistake on their vacation photos."

"Humph!" The snort reflected the disgust on Jack Denton's face. "That's all the questions I have at this time. I'll be talking to you later, though."

Flynn glanced from one to another before he whirled and stormed toward the door. When he'd left, Danielle turned back to the detective. "I want to apologize for Flynn's behavior."

Detective Denton closed his notebook and smiled. "I'm used to it. That's one of the hazards of police work."

Danielle walked around her desk and stuck out her hand. "Thank you for bringing this to our attention." He grasped her hand, and his touch warmed her cool skin. She pulled away and flexed her fingers. "What will you do next?"

He glanced at his watch. "I'll talk to the district attorney. See if we have legal grounds for making Carter take the site down."

"Will you do that today?"

"I don't know. I'm expected in court to testify in a case. I have no idea how long I'll be there, but I'll get back in touch as soon as I know anything."

"Thank you. Do you think you can charge him with anything?"

He shrugged. "I doubt it. He really hasn't broken

any laws. I suppose his dad could say he was just exercising his right to free speech."

She clenched her fists. "Well, his right to free speech has brought back one of the most horrible times in my life."

He said nothing for a moment, and she saw a flicker of sympathy in his eyes. "I'm sorry, Dr. Tyler. We'll do everything we can to get this matter resolved."

"I appreciate that."

As he walked out the door, Danielle thought about the surprising turn her morning had taken. As much as she had tried, for the past ten years, she hadn't been able to put Jennifer's death from her mind, and now it had returned to haunt her even more.

She crossed her arms and hugged herself. Jennifer's murder made no sense when it happened, and ten years later it still didn't. The police had never found any motive for the murder, and they had eventually abandoned it to the cold-case files.

Maybe Flynn's Web site would provide a reason for them to study the murder again. Detective Denton hadn't given any indication the department was willing to reopen the investigation, but something about his demeanor gave her the idea he was a dogged investigator. Maybe he would be the person who would finally shed some light on the nightmare she'd lived with for ten years.

Danielle walked to the door, stepped into the

hallway and gazed at the retreating figure of Jack Denton. Just before he reached the foyer, he turned his head and glanced over his shoulder. His eyes widened as if surprised to see her standing there. For a moment their gazes locked before he turned away and disappeared through the front door.

There was something about the handsome detective that intrigued her. Perhaps it was that momentary flash of sympathy for her feelings she saw in his eyes. Then again, she might be imagining his concern. After all, he knew nothing about her or the devastating events in her life that started with the discovery of Jennifer's body on the mountain trail.

Days went by when she wouldn't think about what had happened. Then something would remind her. Old wounds would be laid bare, and those things best forgotten would resurface. All she could do was pray that she would survive again as she had done so many times before.

Jack Denton climbed into his car and sat there taking in the Webster University campus. The stately, brick buildings surrounded by manicured lawns and ringed by the Appalachians in the background provided a picture of wealth, affluence and privilege, not anything like the small state college he'd attended.

He stared at the Administration Building, which he'd just left. The structure was really a mansion that sat in the middle of a bustling campus. The information he'd read said it had been home to generations of the Webster family before Thaddeus Webster, at the end of World War I, established a university on the property. Today the mansion housed staff offices and classrooms.

The more modern buildings that bordered a rectangular grassy area across the back of the campus looked slightly out of place in the shadow of the main house. He'd read that the newest structure, the Nathan Webster Pavilion for concerts and recitals, had been completed a year before.

Students hurried from one building to another on their way to class. He thought of Danielle Tyler and wondered why she'd returned to work at Webster after going through the trauma of her roommate's death.

Her sea-green eyes had held a sparkle until she saw the site, and he'd been disappointed to see it disappear. He could smell the perfume she wore, and the familiar scent reminded him of another woman from what seemed like another lifetime ago. He grunted in disgust, turned the ignition and punched the play button on the car's CD player.

The music of Jade Dragon, the hottest rock band in history, filled the interior. They'd been his favorite band since his teenage years. Whenever the past threatened to intrude, he could always depend on them to distract his thoughts.

For some reason it didn't seem to work today. Jack sighed and glanced toward the building. In another time of his life, he would have made it his business to find out all he could about the woman with the tantalizing eyes. That person had vanished, though, and had left a shell of a man who was incapable of caring for anyone. There was no time to think about a woman he'd probably never see again. He had a job to do.

He had come to Webster Falls hoping he could find peace in the small mountain community. Instead, he'd encountered a town with an unsolved murder and a Web site depicting a gruesome reenactment of that crime. It was enough to raise the concern of any law enforcement officer.

Was there some evil force that resided in the mountains around Webster Falls? If so, perhaps there were other secrets waiting to be discovered.

TWO

The sun was beginning its descent into the west when Jack walked out of the courthouse. The trial had taken up most of the day. He'd have to talk to the district attorney tomorrow before he went back to see Flynn Carter.

The name of the Webster student brought to mind the woman he'd met earlier in the day. Throughout the day, he'd thought about her from time to time. He gritted his teeth and shook his head. It was ridiculous to dwell on a fleeting encounter. For all he knew she had a husband and children at home.

The idea of home with its frozen meals waiting to be defrosted and the makeshift dinner table in front of the television filled him with sadness. He hated the thought of going to the small apartment tonight and repeating his routine. A stop at the Mountain Mug, home of the best cup of coffee in Webster Falls, could delay that for a little while.

Fifteen minutes later, he stepped up to the counter at the Mountain Mug and ordered a large cup of the dark Colombian coffee he'd come to enjoy. He glanced around the crowded room for an empty table. Most of them were taken by young people engrossed in their computers.

His traveling gaze came to an abrupt stop at the sight of Danielle Tyler, wearing jeans and a Webster sweatshirt, seated toward the back of the room. Her dark hair, pulled up in a ponytail, revealed the earphones of an iPod strapped to her arm. From time to time her head bobbed at the music only she could hear. She stared at the screen of her laptop and sipped from a large mug.

Realizing he was blocking the exit of customers with their orders, he took a step to his left and collided with a man who'd just left the counter. The coffee in his mug sloshed over the sides and onto the floor.

"Watch out." The man's voice rose over the din in the shop.

Convinced everyone in the room had turned to stare, Jack grabbed a napkin from the counter and stooped to wipe up the spot at his feet. "I'm sorry. I didn't see you."

"No harm done." The man gave a quick nod and headed toward a woman seated at a table by the door.

As Jack rose from his squatting position, Danielle looked up. Her lips parted in a smile, and she pulled the earphones out. She looked around at the filled tables and motioned to him. "Detective Denton, come join me."

He started to decline, but there were still no unoccupied tables. Taking a deep breath, he ambled forward and slipped into the offered chair. He set his cup on the table and tried to smile. "I didn't expect to run into you." He nodded toward the iPod. "What are you listening to?"

A smile pulled at her lips. "My favorite rock group, Jade Dragon."

A chuckle rattled in his throat. "It looks like we have something in common. They've been my favorite band since I was a kid."

Her eyes crinkled at the corners, just as they had done earlier today. Then she smiled again, and he suddenly felt at ease. "I'm glad to hear you say that. They're my parents."

The cup almost slipped from his fingers. "You're kidding. Kenny and Mary Tyler are your parents?" He laughed and shook his head. "I can't believe it. I think I have all their CDs."

"So do I." Danielle cleared her throat and straightened in her chair. "But tell me, did you get a chance to talk to the D.A.?"

"No, I didn't get out of court until about fifteen minutes ago. I'll see him tomorrow."

"Good." She leaned over and propped her elbows on the table. "Dr. Newman didn't get back from

Asheville today, but I e-mailed him and Mr. Webster about the site."

"Who's Mr. Webster?"

"He's the chairman of the board. His great-grand-father founded Webster University—gave the land and built the first buildings. Their family has been involved with the school ever since. Nathan is very committed to the school's success. I'm afraid he's going to be upset when he sees the Web site."

"I don't blame him. It's not good publicity for a school."

"No, it's not." She picked up her cup and peered at him over the rim. "I've never seen you in here before, Detective Denton. Do you come often?"

"Several times a week, Dr. Tyler."

She laughed, and the sound tinkled like tiny bells. "Please call me Danielle. I have trouble thinking of myself as anything but a girl who grew up watching her parents perform at rock concerts all across the country."

He crossed his arms on the table, and his mouth crooked into a half smile. "Call me Jack. I'm just a soldier turned deputy sheriff."

She twisted in her seat and pulled one leg up under her. Her head tilted, and her eyes grew large. "Soldier? What did you do?"

"I was in Special Forces. After I got out, I looked for a nice, quiet town and ended up in Webster Falls. It's close to home. My mother lives in Asheville."

She scooted her computer to the side and clasped her hands on the tabletop. "My parents live in Atlanta now. I see them several times a year. It must be nice to live so close you can visit your mother whenever you want."

He averted his gaze and took a sip from his cup. "Yeah. I try to go at least once a month." They sat silent for a few moments. Then he reached for her cup. "Want a refill?"

Her ponytail bobbed up and down as she nodded. "That would be great."

Jack rose and walked away from the table. What was he doing sitting with this woman? He'd talked with her more since he'd walked in the door than he had with any woman in the past three years.

He stopped at the counter and glanced back at Danielle. She smiled at him, and he forced his lips to respond. He should leave. He didn't need any complications in his life, and something told him she could be just that.

The day had produced more surprises than Danielle had experienced in a long time. The last thing she would have expected was to be sitting drinking coffee with Jack Denton. She had to admit, though, there was something about the quiet detective that intrigued her.

"Tell me, Jack…" she began but stopped.

He swallowed the coffee in his mouth and set the cup back on the table. "What?"

"I started to ask you about your family, but I don't want you to think I'm prying."

"No, it's okay." His eyes clouded, and his forehead creased into a small frown. "My mother is my only family. She has Alzheimer's and is in a nursing home in Asheville. That's why I go once a month."

A pang of regret pierced her heart. "I'm sorry, Jack. That must be very painful for you."

Jack nodded. "It is." He cleared his throat and glanced at her. "But what about you? I'm sitting here with you, and for all I know you may have a boyfriend, or even be married."

Another memory she struggled to suppress drifted into her mind. As she'd done so often in the past, she tried to shake it from her head. "No, there's not a man in my life. There was one when I was in Chapel Hill attending graduate school, but he died."

Jack leaned forward. "Oh, I'm sorry. What happened?"

Danielle swallowed before answering. "He was killed during a robbery of his apartment."

"That's terrible. Did the police catch the killer?"

Danielle shook her head. "No. They said there had been an increase in robberies in that area. They decided he must have walked in on a burglary in progress."

Sympathy shone in Jack's eyes. "Then I guess we have something besides Jade Dragon in common. My wife died in a car crash with another man while I was away on special assignment with the army."

Danielle sucked in her breath. "Oh, Jack. I'm so sorry."

Surprise flashed across his face. "I can't believe I said that. You're the first person I've told that to since I came to Webster Falls, and I've only known you one day."

She smiled. "Then maybe this means we're going to be friends."

"Maybe so, but I have to warn you. I don't make friends easily." He leaned forward and crossed his arms on the table. "The way you talk, it seems you've been able to accept what happened in your life. How have you been able to do that?"

Danielle tilted her head and arched her eyebrows. "Oh, I have times when I feel overwhelmed. Two of the people I've loved most in my life, Jennifer and my fiancé, both died, but my faith got me through the bad times. So I try to remember that my life isn't over and God still has plans for me."

Jack cocked an eyebrow. "Faith, huh? Glad it works for you."

His stony expression relayed his skepticism. Danielle shifted in her chair and debated what to say. "It can work for anybody, Jack."

He sighed and pushed back from the table. "Not me." He glanced past her toward the door, and his eyes widened in surprise. "Flynn Carter just walked in, and I recognize the girl with him from the Web site."

Danielle stared in the direction he was looking. She hadn't seen Flynn since early this morning, but his arrival reminded her of his behavior then. "He seems a lot happier now than when he was in my office. I wonder if he's told Tricia about our meeting."

Jack shrugged. "They don't seem to be too concerned, do they?"

Danielle sighed and shook her head. "One thing I've found out about working with college students is they don't tend to get too upset about anything but what's happening at that minute." She glanced at Jack. "Don't get me wrong. We have some great kids at Webster, but they haven't had the life lessons yet that will mold them into the adults they'll become. They're preparing for the world, and they have no idea how tough it can be at times."

Jack studied Flynn and Tricia as they purchased coffee to go. "I hope their little prank doesn't cause them to get some of that experience."

"I do, too." Danielle watched Flynn and Tricia as they disappeared out the door.

After a moment, Jack stood. "I guess I'd better be going. It was nice to see you."

She stuck out her hand. "It was good seeing you. I hope we'll meet again."

He grasped her hand, and his gaze moved over her face. "Maybe we will. I'll probably be back out at the school in a day or so if Carter doesn't take the Web site down." He smiled. "Good night, Danielle."

"Good night, Jack."

He turned and strode toward the door. Danielle watched him go before she picked up her iPod. As she stared at it, she replayed her conversation with Jack Denton in her mind. She'd never talked with anyone who seemed to guard each word like he did, and yet there had been a connection between the two of them.

They shared a love for her parents' music, but there was more. They'd both had a tragedy with the person they loved. The difference was in the fact that Jack couldn't accept what she'd found—faith. If they became friends, perhaps in time she could help him face his difficult memories.

THREE

Danielle sat at her desk the next morning studying a report on students' midterm grades. She ran her finger down the page until she came to Flynn Carter's name. His extracurricular activities hadn't caused any academic problems for him yet. She hoped it remained that way.

Her phone rang, and she picked it up. "Danielle Tyler. May I help you?"

"Danielle." Nathan Webster's soft voice sounded in her ear. "I'm in Jeff's office and Detective Denton is with us. Can you come?"

"I'll be right there." She hung up and pressed her hand against her chest. She knew Jack was coming, but she thought they wouldn't call her to the meeting.

She pulled a compact from her purse and took a quick look at her reflection. Her makeup and hair looked okay. Standing, she smoothed the pants of the new suit she'd put on this morning, straightened her jacket and headed toward the president's office.

Jeff Newman stood from behind his desk as she entered. Nathan Webster, to his left, smiled, but Jack Denton's stony gaze made her wonder where the man she'd spent time with the night before had gone.

She nodded to Nathan and turned her attention to Jeff. "You wanted to see me, Dr. Newman?"

"Yes, Dr. Tyler, have a seat."

Jack pushed a chair toward her, and she sat. He settled into one next to her and leaned toward her. "How are you this morning, Dr. Tyler?"

Her eyebrows arched at the formal tone of his voice. "I'm fine, Detective Denton." She turned back to Jeff. "Have you met with Flynn?"

Jeff nodded. "I'm afraid we got nowhere with him. He insists he hasn't broken any laws, and he refuses to take down the site. He said if we try to force him from school, his father will take us to court."

"Then what are you going to do?"

Nathan Webster's shoulders drooped, and Danielle noticed how tired his eyes appeared this morning. Although in his mid-forties, Danielle had always considered Nathan to be the most handsome man on campus with his brooding good looks and dark complexion.

Nathan glanced from Jeff to Danielle. "If it comes to that, we'll have to let our lawyers handle it. Maybe we should leave it alone for a few days and see if Flynn comes to his senses."

Jack tapped his index finger on the notebook in his lap. "I really doubt he'll do that, but I could be wrong. If he doesn't, maybe the police department can contact the service provider and see if they would ban the site. Of course, Carter might just go to another one."

Jeff's brow wrinkled as he stood and stuck out his hand. "Well, whatever happens, we appreciate your help, Detective."

Jack gripped the hand and nodded to Jeff. He pushed up from his chair and shook Nathan's hand. "I'll be in touch."

Danielle rose and smiled at Jeff. "Thanks for letting me know what happened. Now I'll get back to work if you don't need me for anything else."

She turned and hurried toward the door, but she could sense Jack was right behind. In the hallway she slowed her gait, and he fell into step beside her. He leaned close, and their arms brushed. "It's good to see you again. I enjoyed our time together last night." His soft voice held a hint of reluctance.

"I did, too." They stopped at her office. She opened the door and turned to him. "Maybe we can do it again sometime."

He swallowed. "I'd like that. How about tonight?"

Her forehead wrinkled. "You want me to meet you for coffee tonight?"

He stuck his hand in his pocket and jingled some

coins. "Sorry. You can't read my mind. I meant dinner. How about having dinner with me?"

Danielle smiled. "I'd like that. What time will you pick me up?"

"How about seven o'clock?"

"That will be fine. I live at 295 Pikeville Road. Do you know that area?"

He nodded. "I do. I'll see you then."

Without saying another word, he whirled and hurried down the hall. She watched him go for the second time in two days. He hadn't seemed enthused about asking her out. In fact he'd mumbled so that one would have thought he was being forced to offer the invitation. Jack Denton perplexed her, but she had always been good at solving puzzles, and she intended to find out what made this man tick.

The flame from the flickering candle in the middle of the table cast a honey-colored glow on Danielle's skin. Jack studied her over the rim of his coffee cup as she put the last bite of linguini in her mouth.

When he'd left the Mountain Mug last night, he'd promised himself he would stay away from Danielle Tyler. That idea vanished the minute she walked into Jeff Newman's office earlier in the day. Jack couldn't believe it when he heard himself asking her to dinner, and yet it seemed the natural thing to say.

He had to admit it—Danielle Tyler fascinated him. It wasn't just the fact that she was smart and beautiful. There was something more he still couldn't understand. Perhaps it was the fact that she'd had two tragic losses in her life.

She finished chewing, wiped her mouth with her napkin and smiled. "That was delicious. Thank you for bringing me here tonight."

He glanced at the customers in his favorite Italian restaurant. Soft accordion music drifted across the dining room filled with linen-draped tables. He pushed his plate back and leaned forward, his elbows on the table. "I should be thanking you. You saved me from a lonely frozen dinner in front of the TV."

She laughed. "Then I'm glad I accepted your invitation."

"Would you like a refill?" The waitress stood beside their table with a silver coffeepot.

Jack nodded, and she poured the steaming liquid into their cups. When she'd walked away, Jack directed his attention back to Danielle. "I know you went to school at Webster, but what made you end up working there?"

Danielle sighed and traced the rim of her cup with her finger. "When I graduated, I couldn't get away from this place fast enough. Everywhere I looked I was reminded of Jennifer and what had happened. But I still had good friends here. Nathan had been a fan of my parents, and he took a special interest in me while I was in school. Jeff took over as president my senior year, and I worked in his office some. So they both knew me well. They were very supportive after Jennifer's death."

"I'm sure it was good to have someone to lean on during that time."

"Oh, yes, and even afterward. They kept in touch with me when I went to graduate school because I had received the Webster Scholarship for Graduate Study."

Jack frowned. "What's that?"

"Nathan's grandfather established a scholarship for the graduating senior with the highest grade-point average to attend the graduate institution of his or her choice with all expenses paid."

"And you won?"

Sadness flickered in Danielle's eyes. "Actually Jennifer should have been the winner. After her death, I was next in line. At first I refused to accept, but Nathan and Jeff told me I was being foolish. They said Jennifer would have wanted me to have it. I've always felt guilty because I benefited from her death."

Jack's heart constricted. Before he realized what he was doing, he reached across the table and wrapped his fingers around Danielle's. "They were right to make you take the scholarship."

Tears glimmered in her eyes. "Do you really think so?"

"Of course. I'm sure your friend would have been happy for you."

She smiled and squeezed his hand. "As I mentioned, Jeff and Nathan kept in touch with me while I was getting my master's degree and then my doctorate. In fact they both visited me several times. When they heard about my fiancé's death, they began to hint at my returning to Webster to work. At first I didn't want to do that, but they finally wore me down. So I came back."

"I'm glad you did," Jack whispered. "I might never have met you otherwise."

Danielle glanced down at their intertwined fingers. The ringing of her cell phone interrupted her response. She fished it out of her bag and frowned at the caller ID. "I don't recognize this number." She flipped it open. "Hello."

She listened for a few moments before she glanced at Jack. "It's Flynn Carter. He says Tricia was supposed to meet him two hours ago to drive to Asheville for dinner, but he can't find her. He says he lost his cell phone this afternoon and he's calling from his roommate's phone."

Jack's eyebrows arched. "Ask him when he last saw Tricia."

Danielle relayed the question and then looked at Jack. "He says he saw her at lunch in the cafeteria, then he spent the afternoon in the library. He thinks he lost his phone there. But he's worried because he's called her cell phone for hours, and she hasn't answered." Danielle's eyes grew wide. "What did you say?" she squealed.

Fear flowed across her face. Jack grabbed her arm. "What is it?"

Danielle's lips trembled. "He says there's a message on the Web site that scares him."

"What does it say?"

"It says, *Do you want an encore? Then watch it at Laurel Falls,*" Danielle whispered.

Jack pulled his wallet from his pocket and signaled for the waitress. "Where is Carter now?"

"In his room at the university."

"Tell him to stay there. I'll get an officer and check this out."

Danielle repeated the message and closed the phone. She grabbed her coat and purse and followed Jack from the table.

At the door, she grabbed his arm. "Jack, what do you think this means?"

He halted and shook his head. "I don't know. The message could have been left by some kook that came across the site. But it worries me that Tricia Peterson is missing."

"What will you do?"

"I'll call for backup and head to Laurel Falls."

Danielle pulled her coat on. "I'm going with you."

He debated what to do. After all, she didn't have her car. "You don't need to do that. I can drop you at home before I go out there."

She lifted her chin and directed a determined stare toward him. "Tricia's parents expect the school to keep her safe. If something's happened to her, I need to know."

Jack knew this was one battle he couldn't win. "Okay, but you'll have to stay in my car."

He pulled his cell phone from his pocket and called Dispatch as he and Danielle rushed out of the restaurant. The memory of the girl's body on the Web site flashed into his mind. When he'd first seen it, he had hoped the beautiful girl wasn't really dead. Now he realized it might be too late to repeat that wish.

Two patrol cars drove up to the Laurel Falls Trail parking lot just as Jack and Danielle arrived. Danielle sat up straight in her seat, grabbed his arm and pointed to a red sports car parked at the entrance to a path that led up the mountain. "That's Tricia's car."

"Maybe she hiked up to the falls." He patted her hand. "Don't worry. We'll find her. I'll leave the car key in case you get cold. You can start the car and turn up the heater."

She pulled her coat tighter and shivered. "Thanks."

Jack climbed from his car and nodded to the four deputies who joined him.

One of the officers pushed his hat back on his head. "What we got here, Jack?"

He tilted his head toward the parked sports car. "It

may be nothing, but the girl who owns that car posed for the Web site we've been investigating. She's missing, and a message on the site said to check out Laurel Falls."

The deputies exchanged worried glances and hurried to their cars to get flashlights. When they returned, the officer in charge faced the three other men. "Two of you stay here. With this many police cars in the parking lot, we may have passersby who want to stop. Keep everybody off the trail until we get back." He pointed to the third man. "Come with us."

Jack shivered in the night mountain air as he and the two officers started up the trail. The beams from their flashlights cut through the darkness, lighting the path in front of them.

He waved his flashlight beam to the left, then straight ahead. "You two search up the trail and to the left. I'll take the right side."

They walked in silence for perhaps twenty minutes as they headed deeper into the wilderness that led to Laurel Falls. Jack struggled through the undergrowth that threatened to trip him. As the incline of the path grew gradually steeper, the vegetation became thinner, making it easier to walk. His heart hammered in his chest, and his lungs burned from the high altitude.

The sound of roaring water could be heard in the distance. They were approaching the falls, and they'd found nothing. Maybe Flynn had already found

Tricia, and they were on their way to Asheville. They were probably warmer than he was right now. It was time to call it quits for tonight. If Tricia was still missing in the morning, they could bring in the mountain rescue team to search.

Jack was about to call out to the others that it was time to head back when he saw her. He pushed a low-hanging tree branch out of his face and stopped. Tricia lay just as she had on the Web site. He exhaled and squatted at her feet.

He gagged from the nausea roiling in his stomach, then stood and backed away so as not to disturb the crime scene. He couldn't look away from the still form.

Jennifer McCaslin and now Tricia Peterson. How could he tell Danielle that the nightmare she'd lived with for ten years had returned? He thought of how her body had shaken all the way to Laurel Falls and how frightened she looked when he'd left her at the car.

With a sigh he pulled his cell phone from his pocket and called the officers in the parking lot. Briefly he described what he'd found, asked them to notify head-quarters and cautioned them to be on the lookout for anything suspicious.

As he flipped the cell phone closed, he took a deep breath and called out to the two deputies searching with him. "Over here!"

Within minutes the other two officers joined him. None of them spoke as they stared at the dead girl beside the trail.

Jack turned and started toward the parking lot. "I'll be back shortly," he called over his shoulder.

His feet felt like lead as he trudged down the path. Telling Danielle was going to be the hardest thing he'd ever done. At that moment he wished he didn't know her. It would be so much easier to tell a stranger. In twenty-four hours' time, she was no longer a stranger, and he was about to deliver news she didn't want to hear.

The coat Danielle wore did little to ward off the chill of the October night air as she climbed out of Jack's car. She crossed her arms and hugged herself in an effort to keep warm. Every few seconds she glanced at her watch and wondered when Jack would step from the dense forest.

The two policemen guarding the entrance to the trail watched as she paced back and forth across the asphalt parking lot. After fifteen minutes and no sign of Jack, she approached them. "Have you had any word from Detective Denton yet?"

"Can't tell you anything, ma'am," one of them said.

She pulled the car door open and crawled inside. The only policeman she wanted to see was Jack Denton, and she had no idea how long it would be before he would reappear.

Thirty minutes later Jack was still nowhere to be seen, but other deputies stood all around the parking lot. One after another police cruisers had arrived, and now they lined the roads. The blue lights of the cars blinked in the darkness, and several deputies stood in the road directing traffic to keep cars from stopping.

The scene, so similar to one at the same spot the night of Jennifer's murder, told Danielle that something horrible had happened in the wilderness. She squirmed into a more comfortable position and glanced out the car window. The beam of a flashlight appeared on the path. She sat up straighter and strained to see who was coming out of the forest.

Danielle shoved the door open and ran to Jack before he'd even reached the end of the trail. "Tell me what you found."

The dim light in the parking lot shadowed his face and accented the sadness in his eyes. He licked his lips. "We found Tricia's body."

"W-w-was it like the Web site?" Her lips trembled so she could hardly speak.

He took her arm and guided her across the parking lot. Then he slumped against the side of the car and rubbed his hands over his eyes. "It was horrible."

Danielle remembered how Jennifer's body had looked and how she had reacted. Her concern for Jack suddenly overshadowed her grief for Tricia. Nothing she could do would help the young woman, but Jack needed someone to care about him and what he was feeling.

She reached up and pulled his hand away from his face. Wrapping her fingers around his, she stared up into his face. "I know what you're feeling. I've been there."

The hard lines of his face softened. "I'm a police officer. I'm supposed to be able to see violence and not react. But somehow, I still can't believe what some people are capable of doing."

"You're a man who doesn't share his feelings, but that doesn't mean you don't have any. I can tell you're strong, and you'll be able to do your job."

He straightened and pulled his hand loose. "Thanks. I'm glad I brought you with me tonight." He glanced at the policemen across the lot. "There's nothing you can do here, so I think you should take my car and go to the school. Someone has gone to notify Dr. Newman and Mr. Webster that I'll meet with them at the school in an hour. One of the other officers will drop me off, and I'll see you there."

She thought of the problems this was going to cause the school. "Okay."

Danielle watched Jack as he trudged back up the path into the dense forest and disappeared into the dark before she climbed into his car. As she drove along the winding road, the horror of what had happened began to sink in. She was glad she hadn't seen Tricia's body. She really didn't want to remember her the way she did Jennifer.

Tears filled Danielle's eyes as she remembered seeing Tricia dash across campus on her way to class. They'd often joked about how she could never get anywhere on time. But the spirited young woman had a talent like few Danielle had ever seen. When Tricia sat at the piano, she had the ability to weave lilting melodies and complex harmonies into a performance that transported her listeners on a breathtaking musical experience. Now her gift had been silenced forever.

Danielle shook as tears slid down her face. What kind of monster could end such a beautiful life?

Another thought popped into her mind. According to Jack, Jeff and Nathan were being notified. But what about Flynn? Tricia's death would devastate him.

The aftermath of Jennifer's death had been a nightmare for the school and its students. Now the horror had returned, and they were facing the same situation again.

FOUR

An hour later Jack paused outside Jeff Newman's office. The door was cracked open just enough for Jack to hear inside. He listened for Danielle, but he could only make out Nathan Webster's voice. "I can't believe this has happened. A student murdered? We'll be lucky if we have any applications for next year's freshman class."

"We'll have time to worry about that after we've faced this latest crisis. Now's not the time to discuss next fall," Jeff Newman replied.

"Maybe not for you, but it's my family's endowment that's on the line here. Who'd want to come to a school that can't even protect its students? You'd better be thinking of some way to counter all the bad press we're going to get over this."

A chair scraped on the floor. "Don't worry, Nathan. I will."

Jack raised his fist and knocked. To his surprise Danielle flung the door open. Tears streaked her face.

He cleared his throat and looked past her to Nathan and Jeff. "Excuse me. I hope I'm not interrupting."

Jeff and Nathan turned to face him as Jack walked into the room. Nathan stepped forward. "Come in, Detective Denton. Do you have any news for us?"

Jack shook his head. "I wanted to tell you we won't release Tricia's name until we've notified her parents. I thought you would probably want to talk to them, too. I'll be back in touch in the morning to answer any questions you might have."

Nathan frowned. "Will you have the killer by then?"

Jack shook his head. "I don't know, but I'll do everything I can to assure Tricia's parents that I won't rest until he is found."

Jeff sank down in his desk chair and raised a shaking hand to his forehead. "I can't believe this is happening again. Do you think it's the same murderer?"

Jack shrugged. "We don't know at this point. It could be, or it could be a copycat who saw the Web site."

A groan came from Danielle's direction. "Oh, why did Tricia and Flynn get mixed up in this horrible situation?"

Jack glanced around, and his eyes widened at the paleness of her face. She needed to get out of there. "My partner's gone to bring Flynn Carter to the station. I need to get down there, too, but I'll come back tomorrow." Jack turned to Danielle. "Dr. Tyler, you look like this ordeal has gotten to you. Why don't I take you home?"

Nathan's lips parted, and his eyebrows arched. "Don't you have your car, Danielle?"

Before she could answer, Jack took her by the arm. "We were at dinner when she got Flynn's call."

What Jack interpreted as disapproving looks flashed across Nathan and Jack's faces. Before they could say anything, he steered Danielle out of the room and down the hall. At the building's entrance, he pushed the front door open and stood back for her to exit.

"Thank you," she murmured as she walked outside.

The forlorn hoot of an owl from the distant hills matched the mood that hung over them as he walked beside Danielle to where she'd parked his car. He could almost feel the grief radiating from her body at this latest tragedy, and he felt helpless. Policemen weren't supposed to become emotionally involved in their cases. Although he'd never let anyone know it, he hadn't learned how not to care about those affected by violent crime.

They stopped at the car, and he opened the door. She looked up at him. The tears in her eyes shimmered in the glow from the inside light. Her lips trembled. "Thank you for all your help tonight."

He jammed his hands into his pocket. "Just doing my job."

She started to get in the car, but she turned back to him. "It really hit me on the way back from Laurel Falls. Tricia is dead. Just like Jennifer and Stan."

He frowned. "Stan?"

"My fiancé."

"Oh, I didn't know his name. I'm sorry."

"Stan," she whispered. "Stan Winters. He was a wonderful man."

She looked so vulnerable standing there in the parking lot shadows. A cold wind blew from the distant mountains, and she shivered. The urge to put a protective arm around her shoulders washed over him, and he shoved his hands deeper in his pockets. "Let's get out of here. After all, there is a killer loose."

Her forehead wrinkled, and her gaze darted across the lit area. "And he could be watching us right now." She moved closer to him. "I thought you had to go to the station."

"I'll go after I see you safely home."

She smiled. "Thanks."

Jack waited for her to get inside before he closed the door and walked around to the driver's side. As they pulled out of the parking lot, he turned up the radio, adjusted the heater and tried to concentrate on anything but the woman sitting next to him. It was no use.

As bad as tonight was for her, tomorrow might be worse. He wondered how she would react when she found out that a text message on Tricia's phone asking her to meet him at Laurel Falls had been sent from the phone Flynn said he lost.

The concern Jack felt for Danielle Tyler surprised him. He'd sworn he would never get involved with another woman, and he'd worked hard to perfect the image of a man with no feelings. It scared him to think she might make him want to change his mind.

Danielle studied the streetlights as they drove toward her house. Their beams cut through the interior of Jack's car and cast a protective glow through the interior. Jack's presence beside her comforted her. She didn't want to go home alone. A sadistic killer had surfaced in Webster Falls again, but in the wake of his appearance, she'd met Jack.

Her house came into view, and she sighed with relief. Jack turned into the driveway of the small log cabin where she'd lived for three years and stopped behind her car. The fluid movements of his lean body made her heart skip a beat as he slid from the car and hurried to open her door.

He grasped her arm and helped her climb from the car. Once outside, he continued to hold her, and she leaned against him as he guided her up the steps to the front porch. His muscles rippled, and she recognized a sense of security flow through her. She hadn't felt that in many years.

At the door he released her, and she fumbled with the key. Her hands shook so she couldn't insert it into the lock. Jack leaned over and took the key ring from her hand. "Let me."

In one swift move he unlocked the door and pushed it open. Uncertain what to do, she faced him. "Thanks for seeing me home."

The security light in the yard cast a shadow across his face as he surveyed the surrounding area. "You don't have any close neighbors."

"No. That's what I liked about this place. It's private."

He glanced inside the house and back across the dark yard. "I'm wondering if it's safe for you to be here."

Her heart skipped a beat. "Why?"

He frowned. "Two people close to you have been killed."

Fear raced through her as her gaze flitted toward the shadows around the house. "At the school you said it could be a copycat. What if it's not? What if the person who murdered Jennifer has been here all these years?"

"That's what I hope to find out. But for now, do you want to go to a hotel for the night?"

She closed her eyes and rubbed her forehead. "I don't want to be run out of my home because I'm scared. Besides I have an alarm system." She opened her eyes and glanced into the dark house. "But I was in such a hurry this morning, I didn't set it."

Jack nodded toward the inside. "Want me to go in with you?"

Danielle opened her mouth to refuse. She hadn't invited one person inside in the three years she'd lived here, but the thought of entering the house alone scared her. She pushed the door open and stepped inside. "Come on in. Do you have time for a cup of coffee?"

Jack glanced at his watch. "I have a few minutes before I told my partner I'd be at the police station." His gaze drifted over the small living room. "This is nice."

Danielle turned and smiled. "Come on in the kitchen."

He followed her and sat without speaking at the table while she bustled about trying not to look at him. Suddenly, she felt like a high-school girl desperately wanting to impress her date, but Jack wasn't here because of a date. He wanted to protect her.

When she filled his cup, he looked up her and smiled. "Thanks."

She smiled at the sound of his soft voice. "I really appreciate you coming in with me. I don't think I could have entered this house by myself."

He nodded. "You've had a rough day."

"Yeah."

He leaned forward, his eyes staring into hers. "Are you sure about staying here?"

She realized he would leave soon. She'd be alone. What if the killer knew her? A lump of fear rose in her throat. "I—I think so."

They drank in silence for a few moments. She tried to figure out what thoughts were running through his head, but his expression remained unchanged. After a moment he pulled a notepad from his pocket and wrote something, then pushed the paper across the table. "Here's my cell phone number. Call me if you need someone."

Relief flowed through her. Tears welled in her eyes. "Thank you. I don't mind telling you Tricia's murder has me scared."

His gaze locked with hers, and his eyes softened. Pushing his cup away, he stood. "I'd better be going."

Danielle nodded and followed him to the front door. They reached for the knob at the same time, their fingers touching. He jerked his hand away, and she opened the door. "Thank you again, Jack."

He exhaled. "I'd better go." He stared at her for a moment, then nodded. "Good night, Danielle. Sleep well."

She closed the door and leaned against it. Her life had taken a detour since this morning. One of Webster's most promising students had been murdered, and her school was once again plunged into a horrible nightmare.

Only time would tell if Tricia's murder was related to Jennifer's. At the present time there was no concrete evidence to believe it was, but something told her a killer had returned.

Danielle's breath puffed a vapor mist as she stepped onto the front porch the next morning. It seemed chillier than usual, but she hadn't felt warm since she'd stood in the parking lot at Laurel Falls the night before. She pulled the key from the locked door and turned toward the steps just as a car stopped at the curb.

A smile creased her lips at the sight of Jack crawling from behind the wheel. He walked toward her as she descended the steps. Stopping a few feet away, he smiled. "Thought I'd check to see how you made it last night."

His eyes looked tired, and the stubble of a beard showed on his face. "Have you been up all night?"

He chuckled. "Yeah. Just left the station."

"What about Flynn? How is he?"

Jack shook his head. "Not good. One of the officers drove him back to the dorm last night. We were afraid for him to drive himself because he was so upset."

Even as angry as she'd been at Flynn over the Web site, she knew Tricia's death must have been devastating. "I'll check on him when I get to school. But first, would you like a cup of coffee? There's some in the kitchen."

He shook his head and glanced at his watch. "I'm going home to shower, then I have to get back to work. I'll come out to the school later. I want to look through Tricia's room. See if I can find anything that might point to the murderer."

"Do you need my help?"

"Yeah. I'll call before I come. Now I'd better get going."

Danielle followed him to his car and stood behind him as he pulled the door open. Before he got into the car, he turned and faced her. "Watch your step today. Be suspicious of everybody around you. Don't trust anybody."

A tremor rippled from her legs and swelled as it traveled upward. She swayed toward Jack, and his steadying hand clamped on her arm. Ten years ago with her parents on tour in Europe, she'd faced her friend's death alone. Perhaps this time would be different.

She took a deep breath and straightened. "Thank you. I'll remember your advice."

He stared at her for a moment before he released his hold. "I'll see you later."

Danielle watched his car disappear in the distance before she headed for her Jeep. She'd put off leaving for school long enough. She couldn't ignore her responsibilities there, but today she wished she could go somewhere other than Webster. Jack's words had left her wondering what secrets might be hidden inside the walled campus.

FIVE

Danielle tossed her briefcase onto her desk and dropped down in her chair. Most mornings she couldn't wait to get to her office and begin the day's work. Not today.

The usual happy mood of the students had disappeared. The atmosphere on the campus hung heavy with a veil of fear. The few students she'd encountered on her way from the parking lot walked in groups of twos or threes and cast glances over their shoulders as they headed from one building to another.

She wondered if Jeff had come in yet, but she had no idea how late he and Nathan had stayed. Jeff, who usually was the first one to arrive in the mornings, had probably been at his desk for hours. She pushed up from her chair and strode from her office toward his.

Betty, Jeff's assistant, wasn't at her desk when Danielle stepped into the president's reception area. Just as she started to knock on his office door a voice startled her.

"He's not in there."

Danielle whirled to see Landon Morse, conductor of the school orchestra, standing in the entrance behind her. She sighed in relief. "You scared me."

Landon leaned against the doorjamb. His rumpled suit looked like it hadn't been pressed in weeks, and the bow tie he always wore was missing. "Sorry. Just thought I'd save you the trouble of knocking. I saw Betty in the dining room. She said Jeff would be back at nine o'clock and wanted to meet with the faculty advisory board then."

That meant she and Landon would join Jeff and Nathan to discuss the events of the night. "All right." Danielle took a step back toward him. "Did she say where Jeff went?"

Landon shifted the backpack he carried in one hand to the other. "He went to Nathan's office."

Danielle's eyes widened. "Oh, Nathan's already here? He never gets here this early." Then she frowned, closed her eyes and put her hand to her forehead. "But this isn't like most mornings."

Landon shook his head. "No, it isn't. Too bad about Tricia. It's just like when we were students and Jennifer was killed."

A slight tremor prickled her skin. What was it about Landon that made her uneasy? Maybe she remembered how he'd stayed to himself while they were students and didn't seem to want any company. Why he'd decided in the last few months to seek out her friendship, she didn't know.

Danielle shuddered. "It's too much like Jennifer's murder."

"Yeah. Brings back some bad memories, doesn't it?"

Danielle bit her lip and nodded.

"I've left several messages on your answering machine, but you haven't returned my calls."

She frowned. "I've been busy. Sorry. Is there something you wanted?"

He shook his head. "I just wanted to ask you out."

She walked toward him, but he didn't move. Was he deliberately blocking her exit from the room? "Landon, I'm sorry. You know how I feel."

"Yeah, but don't you think you've used your fiancé's death as an excuse long enough?"

Danielle drew back from him in shock. "That isn't for you to decide. Now please let me pass."

He stared at her without moving. "There is one more thing."

"What?"

"The Christmas Fundraiser Reception. I'll get my students' performance information for the program to you before the day's over so you can get it to the printer."

Danielle gasped. "This isn't the morning to be thinking about that. We've had a student murdered."

Landon chuckled. "Tell that to Jeff and Nathan. I'd

already had calls from both of them this morning about our meeting before I saw Betty. They want to make sure the plans for the fundraiser don't get lost in the middle of a murder investigation."

Danielle could only stare at Landon. After a moment he moved aside, and she hurried past him into the hall. As she entered her office, she glanced over her shoulder, but he wasn't following. She breathed a sigh of relief.

She closed the office door and walked to her desk. Stopping, she stared in confusion at what lay before her. A single red rose with a white ribbon tied around its stem lay next to her computer. A sealed envelope lay next to it.

She slid her letter opener underneath the flap, pulled the card out, and blinked in surprise at the ornate calligraphy that adorned the page. She held the note closer and read—*You have sent light into the darkness of my heart.*

The words sent a chill down her spine. As she stared at the note, her hands began to shake. She'd received a rose the morning after Jennifer's death. There was no card with that one, and at the time she'd assumed it was left by a fellow student. Suddenly the air in the room chilled, and she shivered. Ten years ago she'd felt an evil presence on Webster's campus. Try as she might, she couldn't rid herself of the feeling it had returned.

At nine o'clock Nathan, Jeff and Landon rose from their seats as Danielle walked into Jeff's office.

Nathan, fatigue lining his face, pointed to the chair next to him. "Sit here, Danielle."

The kind tone of his voice poured over her and eased the ache in her heart. She smiled at him and took the offered seat. "Thank you."

He settled next to her and sighed. "We're all having trouble dealing with what happened last night. Perhaps the police will have some news for us today."

Danielle turned in her chair to face him. "Detective Denton came by my house this morning. He'd been at the station all night, but he said an officer brought Flynn back to campus."

Nathan's eyes grew wide, and he stared at her. "The detective visited you at home?"

Danielle's face warmed, and she laced her fingers in her lap. "He only wanted to see how I felt."

Nathan cleared his throat. "That seems strange. You hardly know the man."

Danielle gasped and shrank back in her chair. "He was kind enough to make sure my house was safe last night and to check on me this morning. I appreciate his interest."

Nathan pursed his lips. "Well, when you put it that way, I suppose you're right." Waving his hand in dismissal, he glanced toward Jeff. "Why don't we get on with the reason for this meeting?"

Jeff cleared his throat and shuffled some papers on his desk. "Before we do, I think you should know that

Detective Denton called and said he was coming to search Tricia's room. Security locked it last night, and no one has entered it since her death."

Danielle nodded. "She didn't have a roommate, did she?"

"No, so everything should be just as she left it. Detective Denton said that since you're Dean of Students, he'd like you to accompany him there."

"I'll be glad to go with him."

Jeff smiled. "Good. Betty will give you the key to the room." He hesitated for a moment and glanced at each of them. "The past twenty-four hours have been difficult for all of us at the school. Nathan and I have talked with Tricia's parents. They're flying into Asheville today. We plan to meet them at the airport and drive them here."

Danielle reached for a tissue in her pocket and wiped at the tears pooling in her eyes. "That's kind of you. I'm sure the Petersons will appreciate anything we can do to make this ordeal easier for them."

Nathan leaned back in his chair and crossed his legs. "We've also talked with Flynn Carter. He's all too willing to take the Web site down now, and we've decided to let him stay in school."

Danielle breathed a sigh of relief. "I'm glad you came to this decision. I think he's going to need all of us to get through this."

Nathan's expression softened, and he looked at Danielle. "I know everyone here thinks I'm an ogre, but I feel such responsibility to my family to make this school a success. However, I don't want to lose sight of the people who help to make the school what it is. I'm truly grieved over Tricia Peterson's death and don't want to cause Flynn any more remorse than he probably already feels. Also, Jeff and I plan to do everything in our power to help the police find the killer."

"I'm sure we'll all be relieved when the police know something."

He nodded. "We've dismissed classes for the week, and many of the students have already left campus. There are counselors available for any who stayed and feel the need to talk."

"That's very wise. I'll work with them to make sure the students' needs are met."

Nathan cleared his throat. "I'm sure you're going to help us get through this difficult time. However, in the meantime we have to think about the school. It's imperative that when we resume classes next week the students feel they've returned to a safe and unchanged environment."

"So what do we need to do?" For the first time Landon spoke up. He'd been so quiet Danielle had almost forgotten he was in the room.

Nathan turned his attention to Landon. "We as a

staff have to renew our efforts to continue the traditions we've begun."

Landon nodded. "I'll do everything I can to make that happen, Nathan."

"Good." Nathan stared at him for a moment before he glanced back to Danielle. "We have to make sure this year's fundraiser is the biggest and best we've ever had. I'm depending on you to see that it is."

She pushed up out of her seat. "I thought we were coming here to talk about Tricia's death and how we need to deal with our students' reactions to it. Not the money we expect to raise this year."

Nathan rose and reached for her hand. "Please understand, Danielle. If this school falls short in contributions this year, we may see reductions in programs and staff terminations. I, for one, don't want that to happen. We have to do everything in our power to make it appear that nothing has changed here at Webster. And one way to do that is to assure our donors that their money is going to a stable program. I need you to make sure that's the message we give at the annual fundraiser."

Nathan's words held a plea for help. He'd been there for her many times in the past, and she couldn't refuse his request. "I've loved Webster ever since I entered as a student, and it means even more to me now. I'll do everything I can to make sure this year's fundraiser is the best one ever."

Nathan squeezed her hand, released it and smiled. "Thank you, Danielle. I knew we could count on you."

Danielle glanced at Landon. A wry smile pulled at his lips. The idea of having to work with him filled her with repulsion, but she would do it for Nathan. She backed away. "Now if you'll excuse me, I need to get back to my office."

She hurried from the room and stopped at Betty's desk in the outer office. "I need the key to Tricia's room."

Betty pulled her glasses off and wiped at the tears in her eyes. She held out the key to Danielle. "If there's anything I can do for you, let me know."

Danielle's fingers curled around the cold metal, and she swallowed. "Thanks, Betty."

No other words came to mind, so she hurried from the room. All she could think about was Tricia lying on a mountain path. The people who she thought would have been most concerned with her death only had money on their minds. The idea sickened her.

Pushing the door to her office open, Danielle stopped in surprise at the sight of Flynn Carter sitting in a chair. His body was slumped forward, and his head rested on his crossed arms on her desk. His shoulders shook from the sobs that filled the air. She rushed forward and touched his arm. "Flynn, are you all right?"

He looked up at her, and Danielle had never seen

such anguish in anyone's eyes. With a cry, he turned to her. "Why, Dr. Tyler? Why would anyone do such a thing?"

She knelt beside him and put her arm around his shoulder. "I don't know, Flynn. It's a question I've asked myself for ten years about Jennifer McCaslin's death. Now you're going to have to live with the same questions I have."

He doubled his fists in his lap and gritted his teeth. "But I didn't send that text message."

Danielle frowned. "What text message? I don't know what you're talking about."

"The police told me there was a message on Tricia's phone asking her to meet me at Laurel Falls. It was sent from my phone, but I don't know anything about it. I lost my phone yesterday. Remember? I told you about it."

Danielle nodded. "Yes, you called me from your roommate's phone."

Flynn grabbed her hands, and fresh tears ran down his face as he stared up at her. "Please, Dr. Tyler. Tell the police I wouldn't lie about something like that, and I wouldn't hurt Tricia. I loved her."

Danielle squeezed his hands and smiled. "I know you loved her, Flynn. I've seen the two of you together ever since you were freshmen. I don't believe you would hurt her."

Tears continued to run down his face. "But it's my

fault. I talked her into doing that Web site, and it got her killed."

She thought carefully before she responded. "Tricia should have thought about how dangerous it was before she got involved."

A voice sounded behind them. "That's a good point, Dr. Tyler."

She looked over her shoulder at Jack standing in the open door. She stood up. "Detective Denton, come in."

Flynn rose to stand beside her. He wiped his hands across his cheeks. "Do you know anything?"

Jack shook his head. "Not yet. It's too early in the investigation, but we'll find Tricia's killer."

Anger flashed across Flynn's face. "When you catch him, I wish I could have a few minutes with him. Make him pay for what he did to Tricia."

Jack walked forward and stared at Flynn. "You're feeling guilty, and I can't do anything to take that off your shoulders. When we find the killer, you can't transfer what you feel to him. I'm afraid you're going to have to live with your part in this mess."

Flynn nodded. "You're right. It's all my fault. I'll have to live with that thought."

Flynn bit down on his quivering lip and headed for the door. Before he stepped into the hall, he stopped and turned toward them. He glared at Jack and pointed a shaking finger at him. "I don't care what you believe, I didn't send that text message to Tricia. And you can't prove I did."

Danielle watched him go before she turned to Jack. "I feel so sorry for him."

"I do, too. I don't have any proof, but I tend to believe him about the cell phone, too. I just hope no other students turn up dead because of his Web site."

"So do I." She tilted her head and studied him. "When I first met you, I thought you seemed distant and indifferent, but I think I'm changing my mind. There's a lot more to you than the uncaring policeman you want everyone to believe you are."

His face flushed, and he glanced away from her. "I think we'd better…" He stopped and stared at the rose on her desk. "Where did that come from?"

The uneasy feeling of earlier returned. "It was there when I came in this morning."

"Who sent it?"

Danielle shrugged and walked to the desk. Picking up the card, she handed it to him. "I don't know. This note was with it."

He held the note up and looked at it. When he'd finished, he handed it back to her. "Those are mighty fancy words."

She nodded. "I can't figure out who would have left this for me."

He shrugged. "I wouldn't worry about it. Maybe he's shy and thinks you wouldn't like him. Or maybe it's some old boyfriend who wants to get back with you."

The cold tone of his voice sent shivers down Danielle's spine. The aloof man she'd first met was back, and she wondered where the Jack she'd laughed with at the Mountain Mug had gone. She frowned. "There's no old boyfriend."

He pointed toward the door. "I came to search Tricia's room. Want to come with me?"

"Yes." Thankful to change the subject, she reached for the key. "Security locked her room last night."

She walked past him into the hall, and he followed. As they headed across campus to Tricia's dorm, she couldn't help studying Jack out of the corner of her eye. When she'd first met him, he'd seemed like a hard-hearted man. Last night and this morning he'd given her a glimpse into the private places of his soul, and she liked what she saw. She'd thought the ice inside him was beginning to melt, but now she wasn't so sure. There seemed to be too many layers to him, and she doubted if she would ever dig through to find the real Jack Denton. Maybe it would be best if she didn't even try.

SIX

Danielle turned the key in the lock and pushed the door to Tricia's dorm room open. She stood on the threshold and thought about the talented girl who'd lived here only yesterday but would enter no more. Danielle blinked back the moisture about to spill down her face.

"Are you all right?" Jack asked. The impassive expression on his face held none of the concern for her she'd seen last night.

She straightened her shoulders and pointed down the hallway. "Jennifer and I lived in the second room on the left. I haven't been in this dorm since I've been back at Webster. Just couldn't make myself enter."

"If you'd rather not do this, go back to your office."

She shook her head. "No, I'll be okay. I want to do anything I can to help."

Taking a deep breath, she stepped into the room and flipped the light switch. The cluttered room looked like the living space of a college student. Books lay in stacks on the desk next to a laptop, and the twisted blankets on the bed looked as if Tricia might have jumped from bed and rushed off to class. A bicycle leaned against the wall where a small corkboard hung with pictures displayed of life on the Webster campus.

Jack followed her into the room and stood in the center of the floor looking around. "So this is where she lived."

Danielle nodded. "Where do you want to start?"

He looked toward the desk. "I think I'll go through the desk first." His blue eyes studied her for a moment. "You don't have to stay if you don't want to. My partner's coming to help."

Danielle spied the sheets of music piled to the side of the desk and pointed to it. "Tricia was a piano major. I suppose that's the music she was working on. It belongs to the music library. Do you need to take it, or is it all right for me to return it?"

He picked up the stack and glanced at each of the pieces. With a grin he glanced at her. "I don't know much about classical music."

Danielle pointed to the piece on top. "*Chopin's Nocturne in B Major.* I remember Tricia telling me she was performing this for her senior recital in the spring. I loved to hear her play. She had such a gift for showing the emotion of a piece."

Jack took the music and put it back on the desk. "For the daughter of rock stars, you seem to know a lot about classical music."

She shrugged. "My parents might have been rock musicians, but they were classically trained. We had all types of music in our home."

"They sound like the kind of parents anybody would be lucky to have."

"They're wonderful. Maybe you'll have the chance to meet them someday."

Jack chuckled. "Me meeting Kenny and Mary Tyler. I would never have thought it when I was locked up in my room listening to the radio and pretending to play the guitar along with them."

She grinned. "They're just normal people like everybody else. They live a simple life now on the outskirts of Atlanta."

"I guess they don't seem different to you, but there's nothing normal about them to me. I think of them as rock legends."

Danielle had dealt with opinions about her parents all her life. She only wished the public could know them like she did. "If you'd kept up with them, you might have discovered that a lot of their time is spent working with inner-city kids and telling them about Jesus."

His eyebrows arched. "After all they went through, now they're Christians?"

"Yes. Dad spent some time in rehab, but he kicked his drug habit. He came out with a strong faith, and he and my mother have never looked back. They want young people to know how drugs and alcohol will rob them of their lives. They're the best people I've ever known."

Jack smiled. "I'm happy things turned out so well." He took a deep breath and glanced around the room. "We're not getting anything done standing around talking. I'd better get to work."

Danielle nodded and picked up a book that lay on Tricia's desk. "It's very hard being here and seeing it like she just stepped out for a moment. I hope you find the person who killed her and he pays for what he's done."

Jack shrugged. "No telling when that will be. It's been ten years since Jennifer's death. I hope we don't have a repeat of that."

She'd never considered the fact that Tricia's death would be unsolved like Jennifer's. "You can't let that happen, Jack. You have to find out who did this."

The veil closed over his eyes just as it had done when she first met him, and it chilled her. "I'm going to devote every minute to tracking this guy down."

She took a step back to escape the chill radiating from his body. He didn't have to tell her what he was thinking. She could read it in the muscle that flexed in his jaw. He was letting her know he was backing away before they became any closer. "I hope you find him."

He glanced around the room. "In fact if I want to

get this search over, I should probably be here alone. I'm wasting too much time talking."

She flinched at the abrupt dismissal. "All right. If that's the way you want it. Goodbye, Jack."

"Goodbye." He picked up Tricia's notebook from the desk and began flipping through it.

Danielle waited to see if he was going to say anything else. When he didn't, she ran into the hallway but stopped at the sound of a door opening. Two students exited the room where she and Jennifer had lived. Their giggles drifted toward her as they walked in the opposite direction.

She shook her head to keep from thinking how she and Jennifer had been just like that, friends who shared every secret. She wiped at her eyes and strode toward the exit.

As she reached the door, it opened, and a man with several boxes in his hands stood there. "Good morning. I'm Will Bryson, Detective Jack Denton's partner. I was supposed to meet him here."

"I'm Danielle Tyler, Dean of Students at Webster."

Will Bryson's freckled face beamed at her, and Danielle knew this man was nothing like Jack Denton. From his red hair to the boyish grin, he was an exact opposite of the moody, sullen man she'd just left. Will set the boxes down, propped his arm against the wall and cocked an eyebrow at her. His gaze raked over her.

"Well, now, you're just as pretty as Jack said."

Her eyes grew wide. "I doubt he said that."

Will chuckled. "Maybe not, but he should have."

Danielle tried to smile. "I just left Detective Denton in Tricia's room. It's down this hall on the right. The door's open. You can't miss it."

He studied her for a moment more before concern furrowed his face. "All kidding aside, Jack told me about you and your connection to the two murdered girls. I'm very sorry."

"Thank you, Detective Bryson."

He nodded. "If there's anything I can do to help you get through this, let me know."

Danielle glanced down at the floor. "I'll remember that."

Without waiting for his reply, Danielle brushed past the man and hurried outside. Even though she knew his remarks had probably been a line he used on lots of women, it made her feel good to know that she could still attract a man's attention. She stopped and clenched her fists. The exception seemed to be Jack Denton.

She shook her head. The last thing she needed to be thinking about was Jack Denton. She had too many other things on her mind. Tricia's death had brought back the memories she'd tried to forget of what had happened the last time she saw Jennifer. She wondered what people would think if they knew the truth.

Danielle placed her hands on either side of her head

and closed her eyes. She could see Jennifer standing in their room her hands on her hips the afternoon before she died. She'd accused Danielle of being jealous because she was going to win the Webster graduate scholarship. No amount of reasoning had changed her mind, and Danielle had finally given up.

She still could barely stand to think about the harsh words spoken. If she'd only known that was the last time she would see Jennifer, then she would have kept quiet. Instead Danielle had blasted Jennifer with angry words.

Danielle pressed her hands tighter on her head. How she hoped no one ever found out about the argument, and how she wished she could blot it from her dreams. No matter how hard she tried, she was sentenced to reliving it over and over.

Thirty minutes later Jack still couldn't get Danielle out of his mind. He hadn't wanted to send her away, but he'd found himself concentrating more on her than what he'd come here to do. When she'd started talking about her parents, he understood their different worlds involved more than just her impressive education.

Jack thought of his childhood and the stern father who never had a kind word for him or his mother. Years later when Jack had ranted about his wife dying in the car with another man, it had been his mother who pointed out that in his own marriage he became the man he hated most in the world. And she'd been right.

Shame filled him every time he remembered how soon he'd forgotten the vows he'd spoken on his wedding days. It only took him a few years to transform his wife from a fun-loving and happy woman into an embittered and neglected shell of the girl he'd known.

With him, it had always been the next Special Forces assignment and the adrenaline rush he got from the danger. He'd isolated himself from her and replaced her with his buddies who understood the emotional tightwire they walked in their jobs. It was no wonder she'd turned to another man.

In the months after her death he'd slowly realized that he was his father's son, and his wife had fared no better in her marriage than his mother did.

Jack sank down in the chair at Tricia's desk, and his gaze moved over the papers and objects scattered across the top. He'd been through every drawer, and he'd found nothing that seemed to have any connection to the case. With a sigh he pushed back and glanced up at the bookshelf on the wall above. A yearbook for Webster caught his attention, and he reached up and pulled it down.

"What do you have there?" Will asked.

Jack glanced over his shoulder at Will who was searching through Tricia's closet. "It's the school annual with last year's date on it. I thought it might yield something."

He opened the book, flipped through the first few pages and stopped when Danielle's picture appeared on the faculty page. Her hair was shorter then than now, but her smile was the same. He rubbed his thumb across her mouth.

He thought about the rose he'd seen in her office. His heart constricted at the thought of someone else being interested in Danielle. The words in the note were from a well-educated person, not somebody like him—a cop who barely made it out of college.

His cell phone rang, and Jack pulled it from the clip on his belt. "Hello."

"Jack," Sheriff Chris Peck said, "how's it going?"

"Fine, sir. Will's here with me, and we're going through everything in Tricia's room."

"Good. I wanted to give you some news."

Jack gripped the phone tighter. "What's that, sir?"

"You know we did some checking on all the people who were at Webster at the time of the last murder and this one, too. We found out something interesting about the orchestra teacher, Landon Morse."

Jack's eyebrows arched. "Oh?"

"Yeah, he was fired from his last job at a small college in Texas for stalking a female student. The girl was in some kind of accident, but they never could link Morse to that. Just the stalking."

Jack nodded. "That's interesting. Will and I will be back at the station in an hour. We haven't found anything that points to the killer, but we're bringing a few of her personal items like her calendar, laptop and a notebook."

"Good. See you then."

Jack flipped the phone closed. "It looks like we may have hit pay dirt today."

When he'd finished relating the conversation, Will grinned. "Maybe it won't take too long to solve this case after all." He glanced around at all the scattered items they'd decided to take with them. "Let's get these things boxed up and get on back to the station."

Jack nodded and turned back to the desk. His gaze fell on the yearbook, and he remembered Danielle's picture inside. He picked the book up and placed it in the box with the evidence. He told himself he might need the annual later to look up pictures of students, but in his heart he knew there was only one picture in it that interested him.

SEVEN

Danielle looked down at the steak on her plate, laid her fork aside and glanced at the customers in the restaurant. Soft conversation drifted from the young couple seated next to them. She smiled at the looks the two directed at each other. You could always tell when two people were in love—they seemed more interested in each other than the food.

Across the table Nathan pointed to her plate. "Aren't you hungry, Danielle?"

She sighed. "I suppose I got too interested in studying the customers. I love this restaurant, Nathan. Thanks for bringing me here tonight."

He pushed his plate back and leaned forward, his elbows on the table. "I should be thanking you. It's been a nerve-racking week, and I couldn't stand to think about eating alone tonight. Thanks for joining me."

In the three years since she'd been back at Webster, she and Nathan had often gone to dinner. Usually they discussed school business, but when he'd asked her today, the sad expression on his face told her he needed company. She'd agreed to dinner in the hopes of helping a friend.

In her heart, though, she knew there was another reason. One she couldn't understand. She missed Jack Denton, but in the week since their conversation in Tricia's room he'd made no effort to contact her. Now she sat with another man who'd been her friend for years.

She reached across the table and covered Nathan's hand with hers. "I know it was difficult, but you did a great job of addressing the student body and faculty when we resumed classes on Monday. Your words comforted all of us and got everybody back on course."

He smiled. "I hope so. I didn't know if I could hold up. This horrible situation is a nightmare."

Danielle nodded. "I know. I'm sorry it's presented you with so many problems. I'm here to help you any way I can."

He smiled, but sadness showed in his eyes. "Maybe tonight has helped you, too. You've stayed to yourself too much since you've been back, Danielle. You need to get out more. You have to face Stan's death and get on with your life."

Jack's face flashed into her mind, but she pushed it away. She drew her hand back and picked up her coffee cup. "I don't suppose I'll be getting out much until after Christmas. The fundraiser is going to take up most of my time."

"I know. I really appreciate you taking that job." He smiled. "You know I've always told you that you do a better job than any previous Dean of Students we've ever had."

Danielle laughed and waved her hand in dismissal. "No need to butter me up now. I've already agreed to help with the fundraiser."

The waitress stepped up to the table and pointed to Danielle's plate. "Would you like for me to get that out of your way?" When she'd picked up the dish, she smiled down at Nathan. "Would you care for dessert? Our crème brûlée is very good tonight."

Nathan looked at Danielle. "Want some?"

She shook her head. "Just coffee, thanks."

The waitress returned with a coffeepot and poured some in their cups. As Danielle took her first sip, Nathan spoke again. "Detective Denton came by to see me today."

Danielle gulped and tried to keep from choking. "H-he did? Did he have any news about the investigation?"

"No. He said they haven't heard from the lab reports on Tricia yet. When they do, they may know more."

"Why would it take so long for the medical report to come back?"

"I asked him that, too. He just laughed, or rather grunted I guess you could call it, and said we weren't dealing with a television show that gets its medical results in hours. The Webster Falls Sheriff's Department has to rely on the state lab, and they stay so backed up it could be weeks before they know anything."

Danielle traced her finger around the top of her cup. "How was Detective Denton?"

Nathan set his cup back in the saucer and thought for a moment before he answered. "I don't know. I can't tell much about him. He's a very private person. It's like he doesn't want anybody to get too close to him."

"I had that impression, too." Nathan didn't say anything, and she glanced at him. His dark eyes studied her. "What is it?" she asked.

He frowned. "You're not interested in him, are you?"

Danielle tried to laugh, but it sounded more like choking. "Where did you get that idea?"

"I don't know. Maybe it's how you looked at him the night of Tricia's murder. And the two of you did leave together."

Danielle straightened. "You're imagining things." She reached for her purse. "I really need to get home, Nathan."

He grasped her hand. "Be careful, Danielle. This man will only hurt you. He's not for you."

Her eyes widened, and she stared at Nathan. "You don't have to worry. The last thing I need is to get mixed up with a man like Jack Denton. And besides, he isn't interested in me, either. So you have nothing to worry about."

Nathan relaxed his hold and smiled. "Good. You know I only want what's best for you."

She nodded. "I know. If it hadn't been for you, I don't know how I would have made it through these past few years. Thank you for bringing me back here where people care about me."

"It was my pleasure and the university's gain."

She checked her watch. "I really do need to go home now."

"I'll get the check." He waved at the waitress, and she headed toward their table.

Suddenly Danielle felt hot. The news that Jack had been at Webster, and the fact that he'd ignored her for the past week made her feel faint. She had to get out of there. "I need some air. I'll wait for you outside."

Before Nathan could respond, she rushed through the restaurant and out the front door. Once on the sidewalk she leaned against the side of the building and gasped for breath. Tears burned her eyes, and she thought she might burst out crying any moment. What was the matter with her? She barely knew the man, but in the few times she'd been with him, she sensed something special in him.

"Stop it, Danielle," she hissed. She was acting like a stupid, emotional woman, not a self-assured college dean.

She froze at the touch of a hand on her arm. "Danielle?"

Shock ripped through her body at the sound of Jack's voice. She whirled to face him and then fell back against the side of the building. "Jack, what are you doing here?"

"I came to pick up something to take home. I didn't expect to find you out here alone."

She straightened and pulled away from him. "I needed some fresh air."

His gazed roved over her just like when they had coffee. "Let me take you back inside," he said.

She shook her head. "No, I'm fine. You surprised me. That's all."

"It's good to see you. How have you been?"

"Fine."

"I've thought about you."

If he had thought about her, why hadn't he called? "Nathan told me you were at the university today."

"For a few minutes."

Rain had begun to fall, but she ignored it. "You didn't have time to say hello?"

In the glow from the streetlight, she could see his face, but no emotion betrayed what he was thinking. "I was in a hurry when I left."

Puzzled, she stared at him and shook her head. "I don't understand you."

He frowned. "What do you mean?"

"Since I met you, we've had coffee, been to dinner and been swept into a murder investigation. Yet you act as if we hardly know each other. I thought we were on our way to becoming friends, but I don't think you want that."

He jammed his hands into his pockets and rocked back and forth on his heels. "I'm not good at friendship, Danielle. I don't think you'd be interested in being friends with a guy like me."

The door to the restaurant opened, and Nathan stepped outside. He looked from Danielle to Jack as he walked toward them. "Why, Detective Denton, imagine meeting you here." He turned to Danielle. "Are you all right?"

"I'm fine, Nathan. Jack just stopped to say hello." She pasted a big smile on her face. "It was good to see you. Maybe we'll meet again soon."

She pushed past Jack and strode toward Nathan's car. He caught up with her and reached around her to open the door. "What was that all about?"

She slid into the seat and shook her head. "Nothing. We were just chatting."

Nathan closed the door and crawled in behind the steering wheel. "Are you sure you're all right?"

Danielle nodded and pulled the seat belt across her.

What was it about Jack Denton that intrigued her and infuriated her at the same time? Maybe she felt drawn to him because he seemed so lonely, and she wanted to help him. On the other hand, she was probably better off not becoming friends with him. People close to her tended to end up dead, and she didn't want to lose anyone else.

As the car pulled away, she glanced toward the restaurant. Jack, the pouring rain beating down on him, still stood on the sidewalk. She turned her head and looked the other way.

Jack hardly noticed the rain dripping down his face as he watched the car pull away. Danielle faced straight ahead and didn't turn to glance at him, but he could see her profile. The set of her jaw and the tone of her voice when they'd spoken told him he'd offended her by his seeming indifference.

He slicked his wet hair back and glanced at the restaurant door. Suddenly he wasn't hungry anymore. Instead emptiness filled him and left him feeling more alone than ever. In the last week he'd come to know that sensation well. It came over him every time he thought of Danielle Tyler.

He shook his head. It was better for her if he kept his distance. He would only hurt her like he had everyone else in his life.

Glancing at the restaurant once more, he turned

and walked back to his car. He didn't want to enter and see couples enjoying their time together. Even being alone at home was better than that.

A groan rumbled in his throat. Alone. That's what the future held for him, and it was all his fault.

It had been a restless night for Danielle, and it had been all she could do to drag her tired body out of bed this morning. She pushed the door to her office open, hurried inside, and was about to drop her briefcase on her desk when she saw it. Another red rose with a white ribbon tied around it lay next to her computer.

Her hands shook as she picked up the flower. An envelope lay beside it, and she laid the rose back down, slid the letter opener under the flap, and pulled the card out. *Your eyes warm my heart.*

The phone rang, and she jumped in surprise. The flashing buttons indicated the call was coming from a campus number. She picked up the receiver and held it to her ear. "Hello."

"Dr. Tyler," Jeff's assistant said, "Mr. Webster has called a meeting of the advisory board in Dr. Newman's office."

She glanced back at the rose and swallowed. "When do I need to come?"

"Right now. I'm about to call Landon."

Danielle hesitated. Should she tell someone about the flowers? She'd told Jack, and he'd seemed unconcerned. Perhaps she should keep it to herself for the time being. "I'm on my way."

She replaced the phone in the handset and wondered why they were meeting again today. Hopefully it wasn't about the fundraiser. She had a lot of loose ends to tie up before she could answer many questions about the event.

After giving the rose one last glance and shoving the card in her desk drawer, she trudged from her office and entered the president's reception area. Betty, involved in a phone conversation, motioned for her to go on inside. Pushing the door open, she jerked to a stop. Jack Denton stood to the right of Jeff's desk. His steel-blue eyes reminded her of frosted glass, and she shivered at the scrutiny of his cold gaze.

Jeff turned from talking with Nathan and smiled as she walked in. "Come in, Danielle. Landon's on his way. We'll start whenever he gets here."

Nathan pulled a chair forward. "Sit here, Danielle."

Without speaking, she eased into the chair to Jeff's left and glanced at Jack across the desk. He directed a half smile at her, and she wondered what kept his stony face from cracking into a hundred pieces.

The door opened, and they all turned to see Landon walking in. "Sorry, I'm late. I couldn't get away from some students."

Jeff pointed to a chair in front of his desk. "That's quite all right. Detective Denton came to see me, and

I decided all of you need to hear what he has to say." He sat down and motioned for everyone else to sit.

Danielle glanced around at the group. She had ended up on Jeff's left with Nathan beside her and Landon on the far side of him. Jeff took his seat behind his desk, but Jack continued to stand.

When everyone had settled, Jeff spoke. "I'm going to turn this meeting over to Detective Denton now. There are some developments he wanted to share."

Jack cleared his throat and stood beside Jeff. "I brought a piece of information to Dr. Newman's attention, and he wanted you informed." He held the same notebook Danielle had seen that first morning, and he looked down at it. "Our tech guys have located the origin of the encore message left on Carter's Web site."

Danielle scooted to the edge of her chair. "That's wonderful news."

He shook his head. "You may not think so when I tell you where it is."

She tilted her head and frowned. "What do you mean?"

His gaze drifted over each of them before he answered. "The message was sent from this school."

Nathan bolted from his chair. "What? Are you telling us the killer used one of our computers to send that message?"

Jack nodded. "Yes. Our tech people traced the ISP to Webster University."

Nathan fell back into his seat and gripped the arms of his chair. "Oh, this is horrible news. There's a killer among us, and we don't know who it is."

Danielle reached over and covered Nathan's hand with hers. "I think we knew this might happen. Now we have to help the police find out who it is."

He glanced down at her hand on his and smiled. "Thank you for that voice of reason, Danielle." He looked up at Jack. "We'll cooperate with you any way we can to catch whoever sent that message."

Landon leaned forward in his chair and nodded. "What do we need to do?"

Jack picked up his notebook from Jeff's desk and stuck it under his arm. "We'd like to bring in some experts to check out all the computers on campus. Our guys tell me that even when a message is erased from a computer, it can still be retrieved. With any luck we can locate the one where the message originated. Maybe then we can find witnesses who were nearby at the time."

Danielle let go of Nathan's arm as he stood. "Bring in whoever you need," he said. "You'll have our full cooperation."

Jack nodded. "Thank you, Mr. Webster. I'll call the department and see when they can get here."

He stepped to the side of the room and pulled out his cell phone. Turning his back on them, he punched in a number and raised the phone to his ear. Danielle stared at his broad shoulders for a moment before she turned her attention back to Nathan.

"If you don't need me anymore, I'd better get back to my office."

Nathan grasped her hand and directed an anguished look toward her. "It appears I'm going to need you to do an even better job with the fundraiser, Danielle. This news could devastate our income."

She swallowed and squeezed his hand. "You can depend on me."

"Good."

He released her, and she glanced across the room. Jack had turned back around and was staring at her and Nathan. Embarrassed, she nodded to Jeff and Landon and hurried from the room.

Once in the hall, she took a deep breath. She didn't understand why she was upset that Jack had seen her holding Nathan's hand. After all, he was an old friend who needed her now more than ever, and she wasn't going to let him down. If Jack Denton had a problem with that, then it was just too bad.

She couldn't even start to decipher all the strange signals that Jack gave off when they were together, and she was tired of trying. He was nothing like Stan, and yet she found herself thinking about him at odd times. She was going to have to do something to get her mind off the remote policeman. Perhaps the fundraiser was just the distraction she needed.

EIGHT

Jack struggled with the conflicting emotions tearing at him as he left Jeff Newman's office. He'd told himself before coming to Webster it didn't matter if he saw Danielle or not. When she walked into the room, he knew that wasn't true. She was even more beautiful than she'd been last night when he happened upon her outside the restaurant.

Hoping to see her again, he checked up and down the hallway. Four students clustered in a circle at the far end of the building, and their laughter drifted toward him. It seemed life had returned to normal around Webster. Tricia's death had probably become old news, and everybody was moving on with their lives. He couldn't believe Danielle had.

He stopped in the hallway and stared at her closed office door. He moved closer and read the sign on the wall. He touched her name and skimmed his fingers over it—*Dr. Danielle Tyler, Dean of Students.*

Without warning the door jerked open, and

Danielle, looking over her shoulder, charged into the hall. Before Jack could move out of the way, she plowed into him. He grabbed to steady her, and her expression changed from scared to surprised. She pulled away from him. "Jack. I didn't mean to run over you."

"I was just about to knock."

She regarded him with a skeptical stare. "Did you want something else?"

"Not really."

She took a deep breath. "In that case, I'm very busy. Let me know if there's anything I can do to help the tech people when they come."

She started to push past him, but he propped his hand on the wall to block her way. "It's good to see you, Danielle."

After a moment she sighed. "Much as I hate to admit it, it's good to see you, too."

Relief surged through him at her unexpected answer, and he stepped back. "I'm glad to hear that. Especially after last night. You seemed so angry."

Her face turned crimson, and she glanced down. "I wasn't very nice, was I?"

"You were fine. You were probably just reacting to how I acted the day I searched Tricia's room."

She stared at him. "Maybe we both were a bit childish. But don't worry. I'll be civil to you from now on when I see you." She glanced at her watch with tired eyes. He wondered if she was having as much trouble sleeping as he was. She turned to leave. "I need to talk to food services about our fundraiser event."

He reached for her arm to stop her. "Danielle, wait."

Her gaze went to his hand and up to his eyes. "What is it, Jack?"

He knew the wise thing for him to do was walk away from her, but he couldn't. She had gotten under his skin, and there was no use ignoring it. "Did you find out who sent you the rose?"

She arched an eyebrow. "I still have no idea." She stared at him with the self-assured expression he'd seen the first day they met. Then suddenly, it disappeared, and she sagged against the wall. Her eyes clouded, and he saw fear flicker in them.

He frowned. "What's the matter?"

She glanced up and down the hall before she motioned for him to enter her office. Inside she walked to her desk and pointed at the rose beside the computer. His eyebrows arched as he looked back at her. "Was there another note?"

Danielle nodded, opened the top drawer and pulled the envelope out. "They were here when I came in this morning."

Jack slipped the card out and read the words written in the same ornate script. Did Danielle have an admirer, or was this something more sinister? The guy sounded crazy—maybe crazy in love and then again maybe just crazy. He clenched his jaw and hoped she didn't see how this latest development had shaken him. "Sounds like this guy's really fallen for you."

Her mouth gaped open, and she blinked her eyes. "Fallen for me? Jack, you're a policeman. Don't you think these words are strange?" A look of fear crossed her face. "And there's something else…"

"What?"

"Somebody left me a rose the morning after Jennifer was killed. Nobody has since. Not until Tricia's murder, and now I've had two."

His heart thudded. "You never told me that."

"I didn't think it had anything to do with Tricia's murder. At the time I thought someone was trying to cheer me up about Jennifer."

There might be a connection, but there was no need to alarm her. The thought that Danielle might be in danger, too, made his heart race.

Trying not to convey his sudden concern, he shrugged. "Maybe Nathan left them. Are you involved with him?"

She blinked and looked at him as if he'd lost his mind. "No. Why would you ask that?"

He swallowed. "You were with him last night, and the two of you seemed awfully chummy in our meeting. I think he really cares about you."

Danielle leaned against her desk and crossed her

arms. "Of course he cares about me. He's been my friend for years. But there's no romance between us."

Her words were what he wanted to hear, but he didn't have time to think about that now. He glanced back at the rose. "That still doesn't answer the question of who sent you the roses."

She shivered and pulled her arms tighter. "I don't mind telling you, this has spooked me. I don't like the thought of someone in my office when I'm not here, and I certainly don't like anonymous gifts."

He nodded. "I don't blame you."

She shot him a relieved look. "Really? I was beginning to think I was paranoid."

The roses left after Jennifer's death and now Tricia's could be a coincidence, but his years in law enforcement told him differently. They now knew that the killer had used a Webster computer. That meant he was familiar with the campus. What if he'd decided Danielle was his next victim?

He couldn't abandon her if that was the case. His first responsibility was to see that she remained safe even if her presence invaded his comfort zone. "I told you I don't make friends easily, but with you it's been different. I want us to be friends, but right now more than anything I want to catch the person who murdered Tricia and determine if it's connected to Jennifer's death."

"I want that, too."

"Then maybe you can help me."

Her eyes didn't blink as she stared at him. "How?"

"You were here ten years ago. There may be things you've forgotten that would help the case. Like the roses you received after both murders. I need you to help me."

Danielle's eyes narrowed as she pondered his words. "Do you really think I might be able to remember things that would help solve the case?"

"Yes, but we'd probably have to spend some time together. Would you consider that?" He hoped his face didn't reveal his fear for her safety.

She nodded. "I think I would. Anything to find the killer. What do we do first?"

"I want you to remember everything you can about the events surrounding Jennifer's death. Why don't we have dinner tonight and discuss it?"

She hesitated for a moment before she replied. "All right."

"Good. I'll pick you up about seven."

Her lips pursed. "No, I have a better idea. Since it may take us a while, why don't we eat at my house? I'll cook."

It was one thing to be with her in a crowded restaurant and quite another to be alone. He started to refuse but he couldn't. "Okay. What time?"

"Seven."

Behind him, Jack heard footsteps, and he turned to

see a young woman holding a stack of file folders entering the room. She stopped in surprise and took a step back. "I'm sorry, Dr. Tyler. I didn't mean to intrude."

Danielle waved her into the room. "It's okay. Come on in, April. Detective Denton was just leaving." She turned to Jack. "April is taking over Flynn's duties until he feels up to returning as my student assistant."

Jack nodded toward April. "It's good to meet you, April."

The girl gave him an appraising look that made his face burn as she walked past him to a desk in the corner of the room. "It's nice to meet you, too."

Danielle's mouth twitched. "I'll see you at seven, Jack."

He nodded and walked into the hall. Out of the corner of his eye he spotted movement at the end of the corridor. He jerked his head around in time to see Landon Morse dart around the corner.

Was he watching Danielle's office to see when Jack would leave, or was it a coincidence that he was in the hall? Jack started to go after him but then thought better of it. Landon would deny he was spying on them. Jack still hadn't resolved the matter of Landon's past, but he thought it was time to do so. Landon was too close to Danielle, and if he was a threat, Jack intended to find out.

He thought about what he'd said inside Danielle's

office. For a guy who protested that he didn't want to get involved, he sure didn't act like it. Go to her home for dinner? Why had he accepted the invitation? Aside from his concern for Danielle's safety, he knew he hadn't been this happy in days. He might protest it aloud, but he knew what was in his heart. No doubt about it. Danielle Tyler had him hooked, and it wouldn't take much to reel him in. For her sake he had to make sure that didn't happen.

Danielle was just taking the lasagna from the oven when the doorbell rang. She set the pan on a trivet and hurried toward the door. On the way she paused at the hall mirror to pat her hair into place and check her lipstick. She stared at her reflection and wondered what she was doing. Jack could care less how she looked, and she'd given up trying to impress a man years ago.

When she opened the front door, her heart skipped a beat at the sight of Jack standing there. He didn't have the tired look she'd seen in his eyes earlier that day. He smelled of aftershave, and she couldn't help but smile.

Holding the door back, she motioned him inside. "Come on in. I'm still working on dinner."

He stepped into the living room, closed his eyes and inhaled. "Something smells good."

She laughed. "Lasagna. I'm not a great cook, but

I have a few recipes that I can pull off every once in a while."

"Lasagna sounds great. But then anything beats a frozen dinner."

She nodded toward the kitchen. "Come on in while I finish up. You can keep me company."

Jack followed her into the kitchen and sat down in the chair she indicated. "So, anything exciting happen at Webster today?"

"No." Danielle opened the refrigerator, pulled out a pitcher of iced tea and poured him a glass. She set it in front of him and hurried back to the stove. "Oops, we're going to have burned rolls if I don't get these out."

He took a drink of his tea and watched as she set the pan of rolls on top of the stove. "Is there anything I can do to help?"

Danielle gave a chuckle. "You helping in the kitchen? Somehow I can't picture that."

Jack pushed up from the table. "At least I could set the table."

She smiled and pointed to the cabinet. "Okay. Plates are in there. Silverware in the drawer below."

He snapped a salute in her direction. "Aye-aye, madam. Just watch how good I am."

Danielle turned back to the stove, but she could see, over her shoulder, Jack pulling the dishes from the cabinet. A memory of other times when she and Stan had shared kitchen duties swept over her.

She waited for the sorrow that usually followed, but for some reason it didn't. She concentrated on Stan and tried to remember his face, his mannerisms, but something was wrong.

Stan was fading from her mind. He was beginning to occupy the place in her thoughts that housed past memories. She had no idea when this had happened.

The cabinet door closed with a click, and she glanced at Jack. She wasn't alone tonight like so many others before. Was Jack's presence replacing what she'd held on to for years? She shivered at the thought that this man who guarded his emotions so carefully might become important to her. Jack had given her no indication that their relationship could go any further than friendship, and she was glad. She had to shield her heart carefully. She'd lost too much. She couldn't run the risk of that happening again.

Jack took the last bite of his chocolate cake and pushed the dessert plate away. He rubbed his stomach and sighed in pleasure. "That was the best meal I've had since coming to Webster Falls."

Danielle laughed and stood to clear the table. "And how many years have you been here?"

Jack calculated the time in his head. "Two years I guess. How about you?"

"Three for me."

He shook his head. "I can't believe we've lived in the

same town for two years and haven't run into each other."

She set the dishes in the sink, picked up the coffee-pot and poured them each another cup. "My life has revolved around the school and my church since I've been here."

He took a sip of coffee. "Well, no church for me, but my work has taken up all my time."

Danielle sat down. "I'd be happy for you to go with me anytime. You might find you like it."

"Thanks, but I don't think so. Religion just never has been a part of my life."

A sad look flashed in her eyes. "Why not?"

"I don't think I'd like it. Christians have too many thou-shall-nots in their lives."

She laughed. "When I was a little girl, my mother tried to get me to eat green peas. I resisted because I didn't think I'd like them. One day she laid a few on my mashed potatoes and told me she'd made me a bird's nest. The peas were the bird's eggs. I ate them and discovered I really liked them. I've been eating green peas ever since."

He took another sip of coffee. "And your point is?"

"Maybe you need to look at Christianity in a different way. Focus on the good things that happen to you—like faith and strength and knowing you're never alone."

His eyebrows arched. "And you found that out from eating green peas?"

She picked up her napkin, wadded it into a ball and threw it at him. "No, that was only an illustration. I'm just saying you never know whether or not your pre-conceived ideas are right about something until you test it for yourself. You're incorrigible, Jack Denton."

He studied her closely. He had to admit there was something about Danielle that was different from anyone else he'd ever known. Even with all she'd experienced she had a peace about her. He envied her that. He hadn't known peace in years.

For a moment he wished he was like those college kids he'd seen at Webster earlier today. He wondered what his life would have been if he and Danielle had met when they were younger, before life scarred them. In another place and time, things could have been different.

No wishing could make that come true. They were a product of their experiences, and nothing was going to change that. He came with too much baggage, and he wouldn't wish that on any woman. Especially not Danielle.

NINE

Danielle carried the tray with the coffeepot into the living room and placed it on the table in front of the couch. Jack set their cups beside the pot and sank down on the sofa. He leaned back and closed his eyes.

"I could take a nap after that good meal."

Danielle hadn't seen him so at peace in the time she'd known Jack. His trademark frown was gone tonight. At times she'd wondered why his forehead didn't have permanent lines from the constant scowl. In his relaxed state she had to admit there was something very appealing about Jack Denton.

For the first time she became more aware of the small cowlick at the crown of his head. An impulse to reach out and smooth the dark hair into place overcame her, and she clutched her hands together. She wondered what he had been like as a young boy. Had he shied away from friendships then? She wished she knew what had molded him into the man he'd become.

His eyes fluttered open, and surprise flashed across his face. Embarrassed at having been caught studying him so intently, she sat down, grabbed the coffeepot. He cleared his throat and sat up straight.

"Sorry. I got a little too comfortable."

The cup rattled in the saucer as she picked it up. "I'm sorry if you thought I was staring. I thought you might be going to sleep. I knew I was boring, but I must confess I've never had that effect on a man before."

He set his coffee on the table and smiled. "I'm not bored. Just the opposite. It's nice being here."

She smiled. "And it's good to have you." She took a sip from her cup and settled back in the cushions. "Your tech guys examined the computers in my office today. They didn't tell me anything, but I didn't expect them to. Have they found the computer where the encore message was sent yet?"

Jack shook his head. "Not yet. It's a bigger job than we thought. The school gave us permission to do all the computers that the school owned, but I didn't think about all the students' computers having the ISP of the school. We can't go into dorm rooms and check private property."

Danielle set her cup on the coffee table and nodded. "I never thought of that. So what do you think you'll do?"

Jack took a drink from his cup. "I think they've

probably done all they can at this point. It'll be a stroke of luck if we find that computer."

Danielle pulled her feet up underneath her on the couch and crossed her arms. "So that leaves you with nothing."

"Not necessarily. I wonder if there's something you might remember about Jennifer's murder that could throw some light on this case?"

As it did every time Jennifer's name came up, she recalled the sight of Jennifer's body beside the mountain trail. She closed her eyes, bit down on her lip and willed the fluttering in her chest to stop. When she opened her eyes, Jack was staring at her. She swung her feet to the floor and, after a moment, she looked at him. "What do you want to know about Jennifer's murder?"

The frown she'd come to know wrinkled his forehead. "Tell me about Landon Morse."

Her eyes grew wide. "Landon? Why would you want to know about him?"

Jack shrugged. "I'm just trying to get a feel for all the people who were around when Jennifer died. He was a student, too. What was your impression of him then?"

She thought for a moment before she responded. "Landon has always been a loner. He was a music major and seemed more interested in his violin than anything else. Most of the kids who were musicians hung out together, but he never seemed to have time for anything but practicing."

Jack nodded. "I guess it paid off. He's now the head of the music department at Webster."

"He went to graduate school in the East, then worked somewhere before he came back. Sorta like me." She smiled. "I guess he felt this was home."

Jack swiveled to look at her. "Did he know Jennifer well?"

"I don't think so. Nobody knew Landon well. Of course, we'd speak on campus, and I had a few classes with him. English and history, I think. But on the whole, he seemed to live outside the natural scope of campus life." She hesitated for a moment. "I do remember, though, that he used to appear at the oddest times. I would be in the library studying, and I'd look up. He'd be across the room staring at me. Sometimes when Jennifer and I went into town, I'd see him in the crowd of shoppers."

"Did you ever think he was stalking you?"

Danielle shrugged. "At the time I just thought it was a coincidence."

"Why do you think they hired him at Webster?"

Danielle pursed her lips. "I asked Jeff that once, and he said Landon had made quite a name for himself in the music world. He'd published some original works for violin and piano, and he'd also conducted a community orchestra where he taught."

"What about since you've been back? Have you ever thought Landon was stalking you?"

She shook her head and chuckled. "No, but I'm afraid he still gives me the creeps. I try to appear professional when we're together. He's left messages for me several times wanting to take me out, but I've never responded."

"Do you think he might have sent the roses?"

"It's crossed my mind. I've tried to think of anyone else who was here when Jennifer was murdered, and he seems the likeliest person to have done it. The notes sound a lot like something he would say, but I don't know."

The phone on the table at the end of the couch rang, and Danielle reached for it. "Hello."

"Hello, sugar. How's my girl doing?"

"Daddy," she squealed. "Are you and Mom home?"

"Yep. We got in this afternoon."

"How was the trip?"

"Oh, baby, I wish you could have been with us. I've never seen so much poverty and hunger in my life. We've come back more determined than ever to launch our relief program."

She smiled at the excitement in her father's voice. "And when will that happen?"

"We expect to have all the paperwork done by the first of the year. We're starting our concert tour to raise money in the spring and think our first shipment of food and medicine should happen by the end of next summer."

"Oh, Daddy, that's wonderful. I'm so proud of you."

"There's just one thing that would make it better."

Danielle braced herself for what she knew was coming. "And what's that?"

"For you to be a part of it."

"We've talked about this before, and you know how I—"

"I know. I know," he interrupted. "But, baby, we need you. This could be a family affair. We want you to be the chairman of our nonprofit and deal with all the day-to-day hassle of running the organization. Your mom and I will raise the money and do all the public appearances."

"But I'm happy here."

"Please, darling. Just pray about it before you say no."

She looked at Jack, whose eyes had grown large. "I will. And by the way there's a friend of mine here who's a great fan of yours. His name is Jack Denton. Why don't you say hello?"

"Sure. Put him on."

She pushed the receiver toward Jack, but he held out his hands and shook his head. He mouthed the word *no,* but Danielle giggled and thrust the phone into his hands. "He won't bite. Say hello to my father."

Jack stared at the phone and cleared his throat before he pressed it to his ear. "H-hello." He nodded and glanced at Danielle. "It's good to meet you, too, sir. I've been a big fan of yours for years."

Danielle stifled the giggle she felt bubbling in her throat. She'd seen the same hero worship in her friends all her life, but somehow it didn't seem to fit Jack Denton.

"I'm a policeman," he said.

She rolled her eyes and grimaced. Her father was checking Jack out. She'd also lived with that all her life.

"I'd like that. Maybe we can." He listened for a moment, and Danielle thought his face paled a bit. "I will. It's good to talk with you. Here's Danielle."

He pushed the phone at her, and Danielle put it back to her ear. "Okay, Daddy, what did you say to scare Jack? He looks like a frightened rabbit right now."

Her father laughed. "I just told him that he'd better treat my little girl right, or the whole Jade Dragon band would come after him."

Her face warmed. "Oh, you didn't. You're awful."

"No, I just love my daughter."

She smiled. "I love you, too, and I'll talk to you soon."

"And you'll think about the job?"

"I will. Bye."

She placed the phone in its cradle and turned to Jack. "I'm sorry if my father came across a little strong. I'm his only child, and he's very protective."

Jack shook his head. "Don't be sorry. I think it must be wonderful to have a dad who cares about you. I never had that."

Danielle felt like Jack had just shared the first clue that could give her some insight into his personality. She couldn't imagine what it must be like for a child who isn't loved. "I'm sorry, Jack."

He exhaled. "I got used to it." He glanced at her. "But I got the impression from your conversation that your father is trying to get you to do something."

"He is."

She hadn't told anyone about the decision she was pondering, but it seemed natural to tell Jack. "A year or so ago my parents took a trip to Africa. While they were there, they came across a relief organization that was aiding the Batwa people."

"Batwa? I've never heard of them."

She nodded. "Most people haven't. They're a pygmy race. They're scattered across Africa in various countries, which makes them a minority wherever they live. When the forests where they lived were cleared for agriculture, they became displaced. Most of them are destitute." She smiled. "Of course this was just the kind of situation that fired my parents' determination to help."

"It sounds like a big project."

"It is, but they want to aid the organizations who help the Batwa. They're launching the project right after their record comes out."

Jack sat up straight. "They're making a comeback?"

Danielle laughed. "Well, of sorts. Jade Dragon is now devoted to playing Christian music. They'll be making appearances this summer at Christian gatherings all across the country in hopes of raising money to help the Batwa. They hope their record, along with the concert tour, will bring in a lot of money for their first shipment to Africa at the end of the summer or early fall."

"Wow! And they want you to work with them."

She directed her attention back to her coffee cup and took a drink. The now-cool liquid tasted bitter, and she scrunched her lips together. Setting the cup on the table, she glanced at Jack. He seemed to have taken in every word. "But I don't know," she added. "I'm happy at the school, and I don't want to leave. On the other hand, I'd love to be a part of this with my parents. My dad told me to pray about it before I decide."

He swallowed and looked down at his watch. "I guess you have some heavy decisions to make, and I need to be getting home." He rose and stuck out his hand. "Thanks for dinner, Danielle. Next time I'll treat."

She placed her hand in his, and his fingers tightened. A tremor ran up her arm, and she slipped away from his grasp. "That sounds like an invitation."

He sucked in his breath. "I guess it is. I'll call you."

Dropping her gaze, she hurried to the door and held it open for him to leave. "I'll see you later."

He stepped onto the front porch, turned to face her and gave the half smile she was used to seeing. "I'm glad I got to know more about your parents. You're a mighty lucky woman, Danielle."

Before she could respond, he hurried down the steps and to his car. She watched as he drove away before she closed the door. The evening had been one of the best she'd had in years. Having someone in the house had made it seem more alive, more like a home.

Her parents had often told her that it was time for her to live again, to see what new blessings were waiting for her to experience. Maybe they were right. The thought of putting the problems of the past behind her sent a wave of excitement through her, but the next thought brought her back to reality. A new beginning would have to wait. First there was a killer to catch.

TEN

Danielle pushed her office door open, flipped on the lights and surveyed the room. No rose lay next to her computer this morning. Relieved, she walked to her desk and tossed the briefcase on top.

As she settled into her chair, she chided herself on being so paranoid. Jack's questioning about Landon's actions when she was a student at Webster had troubled her ever since the night before. Long forgotten memories kept popping into her mind—like how Landon used to show up at unexpected times.

She'd be eating with friends in a restaurant, and he'd be watching her from another table. Or she'd be walking across campus, and he'd be leaning against a tree studying her with an intense stare.

Chills ran down her arms. She had thought his behavior strange then and had tried to tell herself he was different now, but he wasn't. There was no denying Landon scared her, and she didn't have one concrete bit of evidence to support her fear.

"Dr. Tyler?"

Startled, Danielle glanced up to see April standing in the open door. She motioned her into the room. "What can I do for you today, April?"

"I was wondering when Flynn's coming back to work. I didn't know how much longer you would need me."

"He said he'd be back the first of next week. His parents flew into Asheville, and they've been staying there all this week. I expect him back Monday, but I really do appreciate all you've done since he's been out."

April dropped into a chair across from Danielle. A sad expression creased her face. "I'm glad to help out. Tricia and Flynn have been good friends ever since our freshman year. I miss Tricia."

The face of the vivacious Tricia flashed in Danielle's mind. She could almost see the young girl running across campus, late to class, and yelling a greeting to everyone she passed. Danielle wondered if that memory would haunt her like the ones she had of Jennifer.

She picked up a pencil from her desk and rolled it between her fingers. "I do, too."

April clasped her hands in her lap and sat silent for a moment. "I saw the Web site, but I don't understand why anybody would do such a horrible thing to her."

Danielle had been trying to answer that question ever since the murder. "None of us can."

April wiped at a tear. "I'll never forget the last time I saw her. She was laughing and looked so happy."

"Was she late to class?"

April chuckled. "She never was on time for anything, but the last time I saw her was the afternoon before she was killed. I was going back to the dorm, and I saw her in the parking lot with Professor Morse."

Danielle sat up straight and grasped the arms of the chair. "She was with Dr. Morse? What time was that?"

"About four o'clock. I remember because I had just gotten out of my chemistry lab."

"What were they doing?"

April shrugged. "They were walking toward his car."

Danielle's chest tightened. "Did she get in the car with him?"

April thought for a moment before she responded. "I saw them stop beside his car, but I don't know if she got in it or not."

Danielle rose and came around the side of her desk. "Did you tell the police this?"

April shook her head. "No. I wasn't questioned, and I didn't think it had anything to with her murder. It was just Dr. Morse."

Danielle stopped beside April and placed her hand on the girl's shoulder. "You have to talk to the police and tell them this."

April's eyes grew wide. "If you think I should, I'll be glad to do it."

Danielle walked back to her desk and pulled her cell phone from her purse. Clicking on the saved number Jack had given her the night Tricia was killed, she smiled what she hoped was an encouraging signal to April. "I'm sorry if I'm overreacting, but I don't think we can allow any information to go unnoticed. The police want—"

A voice on the line interrupted her. "Jack Denton."

"Detective Denton, good morning. This is Danielle Tyler at Webster."

A low chuckle reached her ear. "Good morning. Aren't you being a little formal? Especially since I'm still trying to recover from your father's threat last night."

Danielle's face warmed, and she turned her back on April. "I have a student with me. She has some information I think you need to hear."

"Is this about the murder?" The humorous tone vanished to be replaced by his professional no-nonsense attitude.

"Yes."

"Can you keep her there until I arrive? It should take me about fifteen minutes to get out to the school."

"We'll be waiting in my office."

"Good. See you soon."

She closed the phone. "Detective Denton's coming right now. If you have a class, I'll call your teacher and get you excused."

April shook her head. "I don't have anything until after lunch."

"Good." Danielle walked back to her chair and eased into it. "Until Detective Denton gets here we might as well make the most of the time and get some work done. Did you finish that mailing list I gave you yesterday?"

April stood up. "I still have a few names to enter in the computer. I'll work on that while we're waiting."

Danielle nodded and faced her computer. "I have a report I'm working on, so that should keep me busy."

Within minutes April was engrossed in her work, but Danielle found it difficult to concentrate. She stood, walked to the window behind her desk and looked out at the campus.

She stared across the manicured grounds to the mountains that provided a breathtaking backdrop. The first time she visited the school with her parents, she had thought it the most beautiful place she'd ever seen.

She loved this school, and yet it harbored the worst tragedies of her life. The deaths of Jennifer and Tricia would haunt her for the rest of her life. And then there was Stan. Although he didn't attend school here, he had visited the campus with her once right before his death.

They had walked across the grounds holding hands and laughing as she showed him all the places she'd frequented while a student here. It had been a glorious day, the last fun-filled one they would ever share.

She closed her eyes and concentrated on Stan's face. His picture blurred in her mind. Through the foggy haze that swirled inside her head, the face of Jack Denton emerged clear in her vision. His lips curled in a half smile. All the haunting memories faded from her mind, only to be replaced by a new thought. It scared her to think Jack Denton might become too important in her life.

Fifteen minutes later Danielle still hadn't focused on the report due to Jeff by the end of the day. A tap at the door interrupted her thoughts, and she rose from her chair. "I'll get that. Maybe it's Detective Denton."

When she opened the door, Jack stared at her, the slight smile she'd been thinking of earlier on his lips. "Good morning, Dr. Tyler." A glint in his eye underscored the formal emphasis he put on her name.

"And to you, Detective Denton." She held the door open and waved him into the room. She closed the door behind them and nodded in April's direction. "Do you remember April? She's taking over Flynn's duties until he comes back to school."

"I remember."

April rose and walked around her desk. She held out her hand. "You were here the other day when I came to work. It's good to see you again, Detective."

Jack shook her hand, but when he started to pull

away, April curled her fingers tighter and covered his hand with her other one. Danielle stifled a smile. She should have warned Jack that April had quite a reputation on campus as an aggressive young woman with members of the opposite sex.

With a tug, Jack slipped from her grasp and nodded toward Danielle. "Dr. Tyler tells me you have some information I may find helpful."

"Before you begin," Danielle said, "maybe I should leave. You may not want me overhearing what you and April talk about."

Jack shook his head. "I thought she'd already told you her information."

"She has, but I didn't want to intrude."

"Then I don't see why you should leave."

Danielle nodded. "I'll go get us some coffee in Jeff's office and be right back." She glanced at April. "Would you like some, April?"

April shook her head. "No, thanks. I don't drink coffee."

"I'll take a cup." Jack pulled a chair in front of April's desk and motioned for her to be seated. He opened the notebook he always had with him. "Now, April, what is it you have to tell me?"

Danielle glanced over her shoulder as she reached the door and smiled. April had pulled her chair to the side of her desk and was sitting with her knees almost touching Jack's. Danielle pulled the door closed and stood in the hallway thinking about Jack and their time together the night before. As she got to know him, she found she liked the person that Jack tried so hard to keep hidden.

Her first impression of him had been different, though. That first day they met, *granite* was the word that came to mind as she stared at him. Although he appeared friendly, there was a remoteness about him. Something in his eyes reminded her of the slow-cooling magma that had formed the granite veins running through the surrounding mountains.

She wondered if she would ever know what had fired his soul and left hardened emptiness behind. Perhaps it was the death of his wife. Whatever had scarred him, it had left him with a fear of opening himself up to anyone. She could only pray that he would come to know the strength he could draw from faith in God. Until then, she doubted he would ever trust anyone.

She reached up and tucked a strand of hair behind her ear, straightened her shoulders and walked into the reception area of Jeff Newman's office. "Morning, Betty."

Betty, Jeff's assistant, looked up from replacing the telephone on the handset and motioned for her to enter. "Good morning, Danielle." She inclined her head toward a sideboard on the far wall of the room. "Sally brought coffee and pastries from the dining room. Help yourself."

"Thanks."

"Those blueberry muffins are delicious."

Danielle shook her head, poured two cups from the coffeepot and turned back to Betty. "Detective Denton is speaking with April in my office right now. I just came to get us some coffee."

Betty closed the leather folder with Jeff's official calendar in it. "Oh, before I forget, Landon Morse was looking for you earlier."

Danielle's skin prickled at the mention of Landon. "What does he want?"

Betty propped her elbows on her desk and leaned forward. "I don't know. Maybe he wanted to talk about the Christmas Fundraiser." Betty paused for a moment. "Or maybe he wants to ask you out to dinner again."

Danielle grasped the two cups of coffee tighter and walked back toward Betty's desk. "Oh, I don't think so. But I'll check with him later."

Betty got up and walked around her desk. She stood in thought for a moment before she took off her bifocals and dropped them to dangle from the gold chain encircling her neck. "Jeff has asked you out time after time, and you won't go. Poor Landon can't get you to give him the time of day. It's time you had a life, Danielle. Why won't you at least try one of them?"

Danielle tried to sidestep Betty, but she blocked the

path to the door. If Betty only knew how this conversation was upsetting her. She gave a nervous laugh. "Try one of them? You make it sound like I'm buying a used car."

Betty arched a pencil-thin eyebrow. "You know what I mean. You need to get a social life." She paused, and her lips parted as if she'd just had an important thought. She stepped closer to Danielle. "Or maybe you're not interested in going out with anyone because there's someone else."

Danielle frowned. "Who?"

Betty smiled. "I've noticed that good-looking detective has visited the school on a regular basis. Is there something going on between the two of you?"

Danielle's face grew warm. "Betty, I assure you there's nothing but friendship between Jack and me."

"Aha!" Betty smacked her hands together. "Jack, is it? Since when did you get on such friendly terms with him?"

Danielle felt as if her skin were on fire. She pushed around Betty. "Stop it. There's nothing between us."

"Between who?" Jeff Newman stood in the door from the hallway, a smile on his face.

Danielle glared at Betty and strode toward the doorway. "Betty is giving me a hard time this morning. If you'll excuse me, I need to get back to my office."

"Give Jack my best," Betty called.

"Jack who?" Jeff's voice drifted behind Danielle, and she stopped to hear Betty's response.

"I was just teasing Danielle about being smitten with the handsome Detective Denton."

Jeff gave a disgusted snort. "I'd think she had better taste than that."

Guilt about eavesdropping washed over Danielle, and she hurried across the hall toward her office. She stopped at the door, placed one of the cups in the crook of her arm that held the other cup and opened the door. She could see Jack's profile from where she stood. April was talking, and a muscle in Jack's jaw twitched as he concentrated on her words.

Granite. Danielle recalled the word she had first used to describe him, but now that didn't seem to fit at all. His reaction to seeing Tricia the night she was murdered, his concern for her safety that same night, the enjoyment of a simple meal with her, and the star-struck awe of her parents—all these told her a kind soul with a soft heart lurked somewhere within Jack Denton.

It saddened her to think she might never be able to scrape away the layers and find that hidden person.

He glanced around and smiled when he saw her. Her heartbeat quickened, and she suddenly knew one thing. No matter how long the task of searching out the real Jack, the end results would be worth the wait.

ELEVEN

Jack had breathed a sigh of relief when Danielle arrived with the coffee. Although April had given him some interesting information, the interview had been a challenge. April's flirtatious manner had prevailed throughout. Now April was off to run errands for Danielle, and he could relax.

Danielle took a sip from her cup and directed a mischievous smile at him. "I think you made a conquest, Detective."

Jack waved his hand in dismissal. "I get the feeling I'm not the first one to be the recipient of her charms."

Danielle laughed. "I forget you're a policeman with fine-tuned skills in understanding human nature."

Jack chuckled and reached for his notebook. "I don't know about that, but I'm pretty good at spotting a phony. I imagine April is already gushing over the next male she's encountered."

Danielle's gaze swept over the notebook. She

crossed her arms, and he detected a slight shiver in her body. "What did you think about what she told you?"

"It's definitely something to check out."

"Are you going to see Landon now?"

He shook his head. "I'll call him and ask him to drop by the station. I like to question suspects on my own turf. It gives me an advantage."

Her eyes grew wide. "Suspect? Do you think Landon could be involved in Tricia's death?"

"I don't know. I'll question him and go from there. Now I'd better go back to the station and let you get to work."

She followed him to the door. "Thanks for coming, Jack."

He stopped at the door and turned back to her. "I'm glad you called. I really enjoyed last night."

She smiled. "I did, too."

He pulled the door open but didn't step into the hall. Being this close to Danielle made him feel like a schoolboy, and he didn't want to leave. He took a deep breath and shifted from foot to foot. "Would you like to meet me after work at the Mountain Mug? We could have a cup of coffee, then maybe go some-where for a burger."

"I'd like that very much. I'm done by five. I'll meet you there."

Still looking at Danielle, he stepped into the hallway. "Good. I'll see you…" A gasp reached his ears, and he jerked his head around. He'd plowed right into April, who was about to enter the room. She sagged toward him, and he grabbed her arms to steady her. "April, I'm sorry. I didn't see you."

She smiled up at him. "That's okay, Detective Denton. I should have been watching where I was going."

He cast what he hoped was a help-me-out-of-this-situation glance toward Danielle, and she reached around him and drew April into the room. "April, you need to be more careful around older people. Their reflexes aren't as quick as yours."

He could tell Danielle was thoroughly enjoying every minute of his predicament. Her body practically shook with the laughter she was suppressing. He glared at her and cleared his throat.

"Well, this old policeman has to go. I'll see you later, Dr. Tyler."

She gave a solemn nod. "Five-fifteen at the Mountain Mug."

Jack gripped his notebook and strode toward the exit, embarrassment increasing with each step. Danielle had enjoyed making him squirm. Old people, indeed. Since when did a thirty-two-year-old guy qualify as a senior citizen? He could still run the department's obstacle course faster than any rookie, and his sharp shooter skills were the best on the force. He'd have to inform Danielle that he wasn't ready for retirement yet.

He stormed from the building and hurried toward his car. With each step he thought of how animated her face was and how her eyes had danced with amusement when he tried to extricate himself from April's clutches. His steps grew slower as he remembered her mocking expression and her raised eyebrows.

Jack stopped next to his car. If he was honest, the whole situation had been funny. A young girl coming on to him. And April had been so obvious about it.

A chuckle started in his throat, bubbled upward, and exploded from his mouth. He leaned against the side of the car and laughed. Several students passing by looked at him as if he'd lost his mind, but he didn't care.

Something wonderful had just occurred in his life. He didn't feel as alone as he had, and he knew why. For the first time in years, he'd laughed at himself and enjoyed the feeling. He'd thought it would never happen, and it might not have except for one thing. He'd met Danielle Tyler.

Jack scooted his chair closer to the desk and stared at Landon Morse sitting across from him. The shaggy hair hanging over Landon's ears and the rumpled suit that looked as if it hadn't been pressed in weeks didn't fit Jack's image of a professor at Webster. Neither did the big-framed glasses that kept slipping down his nose. There was nothing about Landon that suggested the professional demeanor of Jeff Newman, Nathan Webster or Danielle.

Jack had kept Landon waiting fifteen minutes after he arrived, but he didn't seem upset. Jack pulled a legal pad from inside his desk and picked up a pen. "Sorry to keep you waiting, Dr. Morse. I appreciate you taking time out of your schedule to come down here today."

Landon shrugged. "No problem. I didn't have any classes this afternoon, but I do have a rehearsal with some students at four o'clock. I'm glad to answer any questions, but I will need to leave shortly."

Jack nodded. "Then let's get started." He shuffled through the pages of the legal pad until he found a blank one. "Now, Dr. Morse, I believe you were a student at Webster when Jennifer McCaslin was murdered. Is that right?"

"Yes."

"How well did you know Jennifer?"

Landon shrugged. "Not very well, but I knew who she was. I kept to myself, wasn't too social, but I saw her around campus a lot."

Jack nodded. "With her roommate, Danielle Tyler?"

"That's right."

"What about Tricia Peterson? Did you know her well?"

"No more than any other student until recently. You

know she was a piano major. She and Flynn were scheduled to play for the Christmas Fundraiser. They were going to perform a piano and violin work that I wrote. I'd been attending some of their rehearsals, so I got to know her better over the last few weeks of her life."

Jack scribbled on the paper. "Is Flynn one of your students?"

Landon shifted in his chair. "Yes. He's a violin major and plays in the orchestra I conduct. He's a very talented young man."

"Did you ever see Flynn demonstrate any violent actions toward Tricia?"

"No."

"Did you ever hear him threaten her?"

Landon's eyes grew large. "No. He seemed to care about her very much."

Jack leaned forward and stared at Landon. "And what about you? Did you have any feelings for her?"

Landon's mouth gaped open, and he half rose from his chair. "What? She was a student."

Jack frowned and glanced down at the pad on his desk. "Well, you knew Julie Travis was a student at your last school, but that didn't keep you from being interested in her."

Landon's face became mottled with rage, and he pulled the glasses from his face. Holding them in one hand, he shook the spectacles in Jack's direction.

"Who told you about that? Have you been snooping in my past?"

"It's a matter of public record, Dr. Morse. You were accused of stalking a student."

A fleck of spittle hung in the corner of Landon's mouth, giving him the appearance of a rabid dog. "Check your facts, Detective. Accused, but not charged."

"Then why don't you tell me your side of the story."

Landon stood up, turned his back on Jack and walked to the one small window in the room. He propped his hands on his hips and stared outside before he put his glasses back on and returned to his seat.

"I'm sorry I got so upset. It happens every time I think about that period of my life."

Jack tossed the pen he held onto his desk, leaned back in his chair and clasped his hands across his stomach. "Then why don't you tell me about it."

Landon nodded. "Along with my other teaching responsibilities I got stuck with teaching the Physics of Music course one year. Being a violin player, I'd always been intrigued with how physics plays a part in the production of tones on instruments. Unfortunately, many of the students weren't."

"And Julie was one of them?"

Landon gave a wry chuckle. "She couldn't understand the first thing I said. So one day she came to my office, batted her big blue eyes at me, and asked if I'd go over the notes she'd taken in class and offer her some more help. When I said yes, she pulled her chair up next to me and spent the next hour hanging on every word I said."

Jack had a mental vision of the unkempt professor and the beautiful young girl. It almost sounded like the way April had acted earlier. He pushed the thought from his mind. "So what happened next?"

"She started coming by every day. Sometimes she'd bring food, and we'd even work through dinner." His eyes took on a faraway look. "I loved to hear her laugh."

"And?"

Landon jerked his attention back to Jack. "Soon it just seemed natural for me to go by her apartment and eat dinner with her. We'd talk about her assignment some and then we'd watch TV. She'd sit close to me on the couch and hold my hand. By the end of the semester I was head over heels in love, and I'd even gotten up the nerve to kiss her. She was the first girl who'd ever paid me any attention, and I wanted to marry her."

"How did she feel about it?"

"She encouraged me. That is until she got her final grade, a C that I padded a lot just to pass her. She came to my office, thanked me for all my help, told me she was going home for the summer and kissed me goodbye. When she didn't take my calls or answer my e-mails, I drove the two hundred miles to her home to find out what was the matter."

Although Jack knew the answer, he had to ask anyway. "What had happened?"

"Her father met me at the door, told me to get off their property. It seems Julie had told them how I had stalked her on campus and how scared she was of me. I couldn't believe it. I could see Julie standing inside the house, and I begged her to tell her father the truth. She just screamed at me to leave her alone and quit following her. Her father was so angry he even turned his dog on me. I had to run for my life when that rottweiler came after me."

"Did they file charges against you?"

Landon nodded. "They called the police in the town where I lived, but the police couldn't find any evidence to support her claims. They never filed any charges. Julie didn't come back to school the next year, and I left when Jeff offered me a job back here."

Jack made a few notes on the legal pad. "It sounds like you had a pretty rough time of it."

Landon shook his head. "It taught me a lesson. Now I keep my distance from students. I remember that I'm the teacher, and I don't cross that line."

Jack pursed his lips and arched an eyebrow. "So what were you doing in the parking lot with Tricia Peterson the afternoon before she was murdered?"

For a moment Landon didn't speak. Then his shoulders sagged, and he pulled off the glasses again. "So you think because of Julie I must have something to do with Tricia's death."

"Not necessarily. We're questioning everyone who saw her that day, and as far as I can tell you were the last one with her. Except for the killer, whoever that may be."

Landon leaned forward, his eyes narrowed. "Do I need a lawyer?"

"Do you want one?"

Landon stood. "I don't think I want to answer any more of your questions until I have an attorney present. Now if you have nothing else, I have a rehearsal to attend."

Before Jack could stop him, Landon strode to the door, opened it and hurried down the hallway. Jack stood behind his desk and thought about what he'd just learned about Landon Morse.

His story about the flirtatious Julie sounded plausible. It could happen to any man working with a young woman who saw herself as a temptress of the opposite sex. His encounter with April earlier in the day led him to believe Landon's story could very well be true.

If it was, then why wouldn't he answer questions about Tricia?

Jack rubbed his chin in thought. Landon could have

been scared because there was more to his relationship with Tricia than he'd indicated. Maybe Landon had become obsessed with Tricia as he'd worked with her and Flynn for the fundraiser.

Jack sighed and put the legal pad with the notes he'd made during the interview in his desk. Landon Morse had just made it to the top of his suspect list in the Tricia Peterson murder. To prove his theory, though, he'd have to find a motive. Maybe the answer lay in what Julie Travis could tell him about her experience with Landon. What she had to say might very well shed some light on two unsolved murders.

TWELVE

Every table in the Mountain Mug appeared occupied by people sipping coffee and staring at their laptops. Nobody looked up as Danielle weaved her way between the tables to the back where Jack sat stirring a cup of coffee.

He looked up and smiled as she dropped into the chair opposite him. "Glad to see you made it."

Danielle pushed a stray lock of hair behind her ear and sighed. "I thought five o'clock would never come. I'm exhausted."

Jack pushed his cup back and stood. "I'll get you a cup of coffee. Maybe that will help."

She nodded. "That would be great."

As Jack headed toward the counter, Danielle couldn't help but notice the woman at the next table glance up from her computer and stare as he walked by. Danielle thought of how April had flirted with Jack earlier and now a strange woman also seemed to be studying him. Although Jack did nothing to attract the attention of women, it was obvious he did.

Her heart thumped as she recognized the unfamiliar sensation that pricked her thoughts. She hadn't felt it in years, but she identified it right away—jealousy.

The realization hit her and she gasped. Why should she resent other women looking at Jack? After all he was a handsome man, and they were nothing more than friends. She still pondered the question when he returned to the table and set a cup of coffee in front of her.

"Here you go."

She straightened in her chair and reached for the steaming mug. "Thanks. I needed this. I've been tied up all day with this fundraiser."

He eased back into his chair. "You mentioned that you were planning it. What's it for?"

Danielle swallowed a sip of the hot liquid before responding. "In early December each year we have a dinner to honor all the donors to the school. It comes right after semester final exams, and everybody's in a good mood with the holidays approaching. It's a big affair with no expense spared. Most of the students have already left campus, but we involve a lot of them who stay until after the fundraiser."

"What do they do?"

"Students from the art department decorate the

dining room and foyer with exhibits of their work. After dinner, students from the music department and the drama program perform." Her eyes misted, and she paused. "Flynn and Tricia were supposed to be on the program together this year."

Jack nodded. "I think you told me that."

She sniffed and pressed a napkin to the corner of her eye. "Anyway, it's a huge night. We have to impress everyone so they'll open their checkbooks and give generously for another year. Nathan has been worried that the media coverage of Tricia's murder may affect the donations, so he wants this fundraiser to be spectacular."

Jack grinned. "I have a feeling he picked the right person to direct it."

His gaze traveled over her face, and her breath caught in her throat. "Tell me that the morning after the gala."

"I will."

She drained the coffee from the mug and picked up her purse. "Now how about that burger you promised me?"

He chuckled and lifted the two cups from the table. "Wait for me at the door while I return these. We need to keep everything tidy so they won't dread seeing us the next time."

Danielle stood up and sidestepped the tables on her way to the exit. Jack's words about their next time here sent ripples of pleasure through her. She stopped at the door and watched him set the cups on the counter and saunter toward her.

He smiled when he caught sight of her, and Danielle recalled how she had thought him aloof and remote when they first met. Each day she found herself liking him more, and that frightened her.

Jack had been up front with her from the beginning about his determination to avoid relationships. If she didn't get control of her feelings, he would likely discontinue their friendship, and she knew that would hurt. She'd already lost too much to let that happen.

Two hours later Jack pulled his car to a stop behind Danielle's in her driveway. He climbed out and hurried forward just as she stepped onto the graveled path that ran beside her house.

She grasped her key ring and located the one for the house. "Thanks for following me home, Jack. I really enjoyed our dinner."

He laughed. "It wasn't much of a meal. Just a burger and fries, but I like to eat at The Copper Kettle. I guess it's a guy place, but I'm glad you liked it."

She walked toward the house, and he fell into step beside her. "The food was good, but so was the company."

They climbed the steps to the front porch, and he waited while she unlocked the door. When she turned to face him, he sucked in his breath at how beautiful she looked in the moonlight. He didn't want the evening to end, but he didn't know what else to do.

Finally he spoke. "I enjoyed the company, too."

She smiled. "From the tone of your voice, I suspect you really didn't want to say that."

He shook his head. "It's hard for me. I've made a habit of cutting myself off from everyone for so long that sometimes I think I must be the most boring person around."

"You don't bore me."

The soft-spoken words stirred him, and he stared at her lips. They looked so inviting, and he could imagine pulling her to him and tasting the sweetness of her mouth. He inched forward. "I didn't mean to get involved with you, Danielle."

She tilted her head up. "Are we involved? I thought we were just friends."

"I don't understand what we are. I just know you've opened the world up to me again, and I'm enjoying every minute of it."

"You have for me, too," she whispered.

He raked his hand through his hair. "I promised myself that I would never allow myself to hurt another woman, and I don't want to do that to you."

She nodded. "I know. After Stan's death, I knew I couldn't stand another loss. I don't want to end up being hurt again."

He exhaled. "Then what are we going to do? There's something happening between the two of us, and it scares me."

Tears glittered in her eyes. "It scares me, too."

He clenched his fists at his side. "Right now I want to kiss you more than anything, but I'm not going to."

She nodded. "I think that's wise. It's not time for that between us. Not yet, and it may never be. We need to give it more time."

He backed away. "When can I see you again?"

She thought for a minute. "Tomorrow's Saturday, and we don't have to work. We could drive over to Gatlinburg. Maybe go to the aquarium. Have dinner somewhere." Her eyes widened at something she'd forgotten. "Oh, Nathan is having a party at his chalet for the staff. I have to go to that. You can go with me."

He stuck his hands in his pockets and chuckled. "Me at a party with intellectuals? I'd be out of place."

She laughed and swatted his arm. "You would not. Besides I'll need somebody to rescue me early from a boring event. How about it?"

The time had come that he had to confess something else he'd never told her. He hesitated, afraid that what he was about to tell her would mean an end to their friendship. "Will there be any alcohol there?"

She frowned. "I suppose so, but I don't drink. So I never pay much attention to that. Why?"

He swallowed. "After my wife's death, I went through a time that I drank a lot. I finally went to Alcoholics Anonymous, and I haven't had a drink since."

"Then you've recovered."

Jack sighed. "The truth is you never recover. That's why we call ourselves alcoholics. We have to fight it every day."

She smiled. "Then I'll help you. I'll be right beside you and drink the same soft drink you do."

He thought for a moment. "In that case, I would love to go to Mr. Stoneface Webster's party."

Danielle burst out laughing. "Stoneface? Have you looked in the mirror lately, Detective Denton? You might find Mr. Webster's not the only one who forgets to smile."

Laughter rumbled from Jack's throat. "Oh, Danielle, I've never met anyone like you. I think you're good for me."

"Then will you go?"

He thought for a moment. "What time?"

"We need to be there about four o'clock. It's a come-and-go type thing. We can make an appearance, sample the appetizers, and leave because we have dinner reservations in Gatlinburg."

He cocked an eyebrow. "Do we have reservations?"

She smiled. "We do if you make them tomorrow."

He laughed. "All right. I'll pick you up about three-thirty, and we'll go to Mr. Webster's party. See you then."

She opened the door, stepped inside and turned to face him. "Good night, Jack. I had a wonderful time."

His chest tightened and he struggled to smile. "I did, too, Danielle. See you tomorrow."

She closed the door, and he stood there thinking about his evening. Their dinner might not have been at the fanciest restaurant in town, but there was no denying how much he enjoyed the evening.

His confession about his previous drinking problem didn't seem to worry her either. He wondered if the faith she talked about helped her to accept people and their flaws without being judgmental. If it did, then maybe he could learn something from her. Not that he could ever see himself becoming a believer, but he had to admit she had something he'd never encountered in anyone else.

As he got to know her, he found they shared other things in common. Tonight at dinner they'd talked about their likes and dislikes, and he'd been surprised to find out that she liked baseball almost as much as he did. He smiled and hopped down the steps.

He jumped in his car and turned the ignition. What a day! He'd laughed for the first time in a while and he'd almost kissed a woman. The memory of Danielle standing in the moonlight returned as he backed the car from the driveway. This might not have been the right time for a kiss, but he felt sure there would be the perfect moment in the future.

* * *

Jack took a sip of his ginger ale and glanced around at the people spread across Nathan Webster's formal dining room and the huge living room beyond. When Danielle had said chalet, he expected a rustic cabin tucked in the mountains, not this huge mansion that towered among the maple and pine trees at the end of a gated trail. When they'd first driven up, he thought they must have come to a lodge, not a home where a man lived alone.

Danielle smiled up at him. "Enjoying yourself?"

Jack chuckled. "So this is how the rich and famous live?"

She raised her glass of ginger ale to her mouth. "I don't know about that. Everybody here, with the exception of Nathan, is a faculty member just like me."

He let his gaze rove over the group of mostly middle-aged men and women and grinned. Even if he hadn't known, he could've guessed their occupations. Each one of them had an academic look about them. Maybe it was their dark-colored clothes or perhaps the impression of high IQs they projected that he'd come to associate with the teaching profession. All of them looked the part. All of them except Danielle.

He smiled at her. "They may be faculty members, but there's not one here like you." Color rose in her cheeks. "How many teachers are there at Webster?"

She thought a moment. "I think at the beginning of the year we had over ninety."

Jack's eyebrows raised in surprise. "Ninety? For four hundred students?"

Danielle nodded. "When the Webster family endowed the school, they wanted only the most gifted students. So they offered full scholarships to anyone with high SAT scores who could pass the difficult entrance exams. They also wanted to keep the enrollment low and faculty numbers high so there would be more one-on-one attention to the students."

"And you were one of those that got in."

Danielle glanced across the room at Nathan. "Yeah, but it wasn't easy. Even after I passed the exams, the screening committee was still reluctant to admit me."

Jack's mouth gaped open. "You've got to be kidding. Why?"

She set her glass down on a table beside her and chuckled. "Nathan had been a fan of my parents and knew about their drug and alcohol abuse. He thought I might be tainted because of my heritage."

"So how did you get in?"

"The committee invited me for an interview. I was so scared when I walked into that room. But from the minute Nathan met me, he liked me. The interview was a success, and Nathan became one of my best friends. I don't know what I would have done without him after Jennifer's and Stan's deaths."

Jack thought of seeing Danielle with Nathan at the restaurant and tried to ignore the twinge of jealousy that nibbled at his mind. "He seemed to be very attentive the night I saw him with you at the restaurant."

Her eyes grew wide. "Like I said, he's been a wonderful friend."

Jack took a sip from his glass. He groaned as Nathan Webster, who'd been circulating about the room and chatting with his guests, spied them standing in the dining room and headed in their direction. "Here comes Stoneface now."

Danielle frowned at Jack and held out her hand. "Nathan, what a wonderful party. Thank you so much for inviting me."

Nathan cupped Danielle's hand in both of his and smiled. "I'm so glad you're enjoying it, Danielle." He released her fingers and shook Jack's hand. "Detective Denton, I'm happy you could join us."

Jack cut his eyes toward Danielle. "Danielle invited me."

Nathan smiled. "I didn't realize you had become such good friends."

"Danielle's been helping me with the case."

Danielle looked up at Jack, a hint of surprise on her face.

Nathan leaned closer. "Do you have any leads that you can share with me? We're eager for this sad affair to be brought to a close."

Jack shook his head. "Nothing yet, but maybe soon."

Nathan pursed his lips. "That's disappointing." After a moment he exhaled and turned to Danielle. "I spoke to the food services director, and he told me he's very impressed with the menu you chose for the fundraiser. I knew I'd put the right person in charge when I chose you."

Jack nodded as Nathan turned and walked away. Danielle watched him before she turned back to Jack. "Did you hear that? He liked what I chose. I was afraid he'd want something different."

Jack smiled at her. "I'm not surprised that he was pleased. You're successful at everything you do."

Across the room a man motioned to Danielle, and she placed her hand on Jack's arm. "Could you excuse me a moment? I need to speak to Dr. Cranston. I'll be right back."

Jack watched as Danielle walked toward the paunchy man standing with a group of university faculty. They smiled and nodded as she approached. Within minutes she was involved in an animated conversation with them.

As he studied her face, he noticed the ease with which she fit into the group. This was her life. Two men walked by him, and he heard one of them say "derivative formula." He had no idea what they were talking about.

Jack glanced around the room and realized this scene was far from anything he'd ever known. Conversations with intellectuals seemed foreign to him, and he wondered what he was doing here.

Suddenly he wanted to leave, to have Danielle to himself. But with that thought came the realization of his selfishness. Maybe he didn't fit in, but Danielle did. This was her world, but it was far from his. He'd been deluding himself that they could overcome the differences between them, but now he knew they couldn't. Sadness like he'd never known flowed through him.

Danielle backed away from the group and strode back to where he waited. "We can go now if you want."

Jack gave a curt nod. "Good. You say your goodbyes, and I'll get our coats."

Without waiting for her to answer he headed toward the den at the back of the house and retrieved the coats they'd left there upon arriving. He turned and walked toward the door but hesitated at the sound of footsteps in the hallway. Not eager to start a conversation with another intellectual, Jack stepped behind the open door to keep from being seen.

"I was surprised to see Danielle with that policeman."

Jack's eyebrows arched at the sound of Nathan Webster's voice.

"I know. I didn't realize she was seeing him," Jeff Newman replied.

"Have you told her about the promotion yet?" Jack pressed his ear closer to the door to catch Nathan's words.

"I haven't. I thought I'd wait until after the fund-raiser."

The sound of fingernails tapping on a glass drifted through the door. When they quieted, Nathan spoke again. "To be vice president of Webster is quite an accomplishment for a woman her age. If she's become infatuated with Detective Denton, I hope she doesn't lose sight of what's best for her professionally."

"Surely she wouldn't do that." Jeff's voice sounded worried. "She's worked for years to get an opportunity like this."

Nathan sighed. "Maybe we shouldn't wait until the new year to tell her. Go on and talk to her Monday morning." The ice in the glass tinkled as if it was being swirled about. "When you offer her the job, perhaps you'd better remind her that she needs a man in her life who understands the academic life. Jack Denton obviously doesn't."

"I will."

The men moved away from the door, and Jack stood there replaying what they'd said. It was clear they didn't want Danielle's relationship with him to destroy her chance at a promotion. He didn't want that, either.

Jack clutched the coats tighter and hurried from the room. He spied Danielle standing near the front door. Landon Morse, his attention directed to Danielle, smiled down at her as she talked. Landon glanced up as Jack approached.

Landon's eyes burned with a smoldering fury as Jack stopped next to Danielle. "Detective Denton," he said, "imagine meeting you here."

The dislike for the man that Jack had felt the first time he met him rose in Jack's throat. He still considered Landon a chief suspect in Tricia Peterson's death. He thought of their conversation in his office and the report on his desk that told of Landon's stalking a female student at the school where he'd previously been employed.

Jack felt his eyes grow wide. He shouldn't be pointing the finger of guilt at anyone. Not with his guilt over his shortcomings as a husband. If it wasn't for him, his wife would never have turned to another man and would still be alive. He swallowed and forced himself to speak. "We were just leaving, Dr. Morse."

Landon glanced at him. "That's what Danielle said. I suppose we are a boring group to somebody who's used to chasing criminals."

Jack glanced around the room. "You never can tell who may be hiding in a crowd. One thing I've learned since coming to Webster Falls is that a lot of people have secrets."

Landon's face mottled with rage, and Danielle stepped between them. "Would you help me with my coat, Jack?"

"Sure." Jack pulled his attention away from Landon and held the coat while she slipped it on.

Danielle took a deep breath. "I'll see you Monday, Landon."

He nodded, then turned a somber stare toward Jack. "Goodbye, Detective Denton."

Without speaking, Jack took Danielle's arm and steered her to the door. Once outside he inhaled, and the fresh air calmed him. It had been evident from the minute he walked in the door of Nathan Webster's house that he was out of his league. He didn't understand any of the conversation around him, and he'd been ignored by most of the people in attendance.

He'd been wrong to come. He would have been more comfortable sitting in front of the TV watching a ball game than being in that bunch of people.

When they were settled in the car, Danielle snuggled back in the seat and sighed. "That was fun, wasn't it? I'm glad we came."

Jack gave a grunt of disgust. "I've had more fun questioning the suspect in a murder than I did with those snobs."

Danielle sat up straight and turned to stare at him. "Snobs? I thought everyone was very nice to you."

A cynical laugh came from Jack's throat. "Yeah,

nice to you. It was evident from the minute I walked in they thought I was way out of my league."

Danielle's eyes grew wider. "You're imagining that."

Nathan and Jeff's words flashed into his mind, and he pounded his fists on the steering wheel. "I didn't imagine what I overheard your two bosses say about you being there with *that policeman*. They said it like it was dirty."

Danielle reached out to him. "Oh, Jack, I'm sorry."

He drew back from her touch and faced her. "They made it very evident that any relationship with me might cost you a promotion in your job."

She frowned. "What kind of promotion?"

Guilt flowed through him at the thought he might tell her the surprise they were planning. "It doesn't matter. They made it plain that I'm not suitable for their circle."

Danielle swiveled in her seat toward him. "I can't believe they would say something like that."

"Well, they did, and the funny thing is that they're right. With all the baggage I have, there's no way I can have a friendship, much less a relationship, with a woman. It's better to find it out now than later I guess."

Her chin quivered. "Are you saying that you don't want to see me anymore?"

He turned the ignition and put the gearshift into Reverse. Looking over his shoulder, he backed from the parking spot into the road, stopped, and shifted into Drive.

"Yeah, I guess that's what I'm saying. Better to stop now than end up with both of us getting hurt." He turned toward her and he could see the pain he'd just caused her. He gripped the steering wheel to keep from reaching for her. "I think we'd better forget dinner in Gatlinburg. I'll take you home."

She turned her face away and stared out the window. With a sigh he eased down on the accelerator and drove onto the mountain road toward Webster Falls. Neither of them spoke all the way to town.

When he pulled up in front of her house, she opened the door and bolted for the porch before he could get out. He sat in the car as she disappeared into the log cabin. His heart cried for him to follow her, but his head told him it was no use. All along he'd known how it would end, and he'd been right.

Nothing in his life had ever worked out. Danielle Tyler was as lost to him as everything else he'd ever wanted.

THIRTEEN

Danielle sat at her desk on Monday morning and stared at the red rose that lay beside her computer. The card, written in the same script, sent chills down her spine. She picked it up and read it again. *Beauty surrounds you wherever you go.*

She reached for the phone again to call Jack but pulled her hand back. What would she say? That she'd received another anonymous rose, and he would remind her she had nothing to worry about. She'd caught the attention of someone too shy to express his feelings.

In her heart Danielle knew the answer had to be something more. The notes sounded like lines from poems, but they could have been written by the sender. If she was to discover the identity of the sender, she'd have to do it alone. After Saturday night she doubted she'd be seeing Jack anymore.

Their conversation still haunted her. One minute they seemed to be enjoying the party, and the next

Jack was ranting about snobs and promotions. His statement about having too much baggage to ever have a relationship with a woman troubled her most.

She got up from her desk and walked to the window. She stared at the mountains. Once those majestic peaks had thrilled her, but now every time she looked at them she thought of Jennifer and Tricia. The hills hid the secret to their murders, but they weren't divulging it. Not yet anyway.

The phone rang, and she turned and picked it up. "Danielle Tyler. May I help you?"

"Danielle, this is Betty. Dr. Newman wants to see you in his office. Can you come?"

"I'll be right there."

She hung up the phone and walked toward the door. Just as she reached it, a soft knock sounded from the other side. Opening the door, she sucked in her breath at the sight of Flynn Carter standing in the hallway.

His usual tan had faded, and his pale face looked as if he hadn't slept in days. The once cocky student who'd defied the police about his Web site looked like a broken person. His shoulders drooped, and his hair tumbled across his forehead.

Flynn stuck his hands in his pockets and stood without speaking as Danielle's gaze drifted over him. She tried to ignore the anger that burned in the pit of her stomach.

Tricia might still be alive if Flynn hadn't persuaded

her to pose for that Web site. That thought had entered her mind often during the past few weeks, and she wanted to rid herself of such ideas. She concentrated on the grief that radiated from Flynn and tried to understand what he was feeling.

Danielle reached out and drew him into her office. "Flynn, it's good to see you. How are you?"

He shoved his hands in his pocket. "I've been better." His chin quivered so that Danielle wondered how he spoke.

She smiled. "Well, it's good to see you back at school. I've missed you. April has been doing your work, but she needs a lot of supervision."

He rocked back and forth from his toes to his heels and blinked at the tears in his eyes. "I came by to tell you I can't come back to work for a while. I don't even know if I'm going to be able to finish this semester."

Danielle took hold of his arm and guided him to a chair. With his chin touching his chest he slouched in the seat. After a moment he raised his head and looked at her.

"Flynn, I know how you're feeling. I felt the same when Jennifer was killed, but you can't let this ruin your life. Tricia wouldn't want that."

A tear escaped his eye, and he wiped it away. "I can't think of anything but her. I loved her, Dr. Tyler, but I can't get past this guilt that I'm responsible for her death. If I hadn't asked her to pose for that Web site…"

Danielle shook her head. "You can't dwell on that. You have to go on with your life. It's not easy, but it can be done."

He clasped his hands in his lap. "I don't think I can stay here."

"The semester's almost over. We're well into November, and finals are coming up the first of December. Thanksgiving break will give you some time off. So we're only talking about a few weeks. Don't throw away a whole semester's work with such little time left."

He sat in thought before he answered. "I guess you're right. I'll try, but I don't know if I can do it." He took a deep breath. "Do you think April could keep working for you? I don't think I can do the job and classwork."

Danielle stood, and he rose from his chair. "Don't worry about the job. We'll make it fine. After Christmas if you feel like resuming the responsibilities of my assistant, you can come back then."

A weak smile pulled at his lips. "Thanks, Dr. Tyler. I'm sorry for all the problems I've caused."

She placed her hand on his shoulder. "I know you are. Now go on to class. Get back in the routine. It'll be good for you."

Biting his lip, he nodded and walked from the room. Danielle watched as he trudged down the hall. Flynn's hunched figure looked as if he carried the weight of the world on his shoulders. She'd felt the same way after Jennifer's murder. Those feelings, though, didn't compare to the grief she felt when Stan died.

The face of Jack Denton materialized in her mind. Three nights ago they'd laughed and talked, and she'd felt herself drawn to him. Those hopes had been dashed the next night by his curt dismissal of her. Perhaps he'd been right when he'd said it was better to end it before it went any further.

Danielle glanced in the direction of Jeff's office and gasped. With Flynn's arrival, she'd forgotten all about Betty's call. She hurried across the hall and into the reception area of the president's office.

Betty looked up from her computer. "I thought I was going to have to call you again."

"I'm sorry. Flynn Carter came by my office."

Betty took off her glasses and let them dangle on the attached chain. "How is he?"

Danielle shook her head. "Not good. He wants to drop out of school, but I think I convinced him to stay until the end of the semester."

"Good." Betty tilted her head toward Jeff's door. "He's expecting you. Just go on in."

"Thanks, Betty." She stopped at the door and tapped before entering.

Jeff rose from his chair behind his desk as she entered his office. "Come in, Danielle. How are you this morning?"

He motioned to a chair, and she sank into it. "I'm

fine. I would have come sooner, but Flynn came by my office."

"How is he?"

"Not good. He looks terrible, and I think he feels worse. He wants to drop out of school."

Jeff's eyes widened in surprise. "Now? This close to the end of the semester?"

Danielle nodded. "I think I convinced him to stay, but I'm not sure."

"Maybe I need to talk to him."

"Oh, Jeff, that would be great. Let him know that we only want what's best for him."

"I will." Jeff picked up a pen from his desk and rolled it between his fingers. He stared at it for a moment before he glanced up. "I want what's best for all the students and faculty at Webster."

"I've always known that, Jeff."

He took a deep breath. "There's no one I want it for more than you, Danielle. You've become very special to me."

The tone of his words reminded her of thick syrup as they poured over her, and she fidgeted in discomfort at his intense stare. "Wh-what do you mean?"

Jeff dropped the pen, leaned forward and clasped his hands on his desk. "You have a bright future here at Webster. Nathan and I are very pleased with the work you do. We don't want to see you do anything to jeopardize that."

The memory of Jack's words about what Nathan and Jeff said about him returned, and her heart pounded. Could Jack have been right in what he heard? She sat up straight. "What are you trying to say, Jeff?"

He shrugged. "I'm just saying that Nathan and I have big plans for you." He smiled. "I called you in here to tell you that after the first of the year we're making you vice president of the college. You'll be moving into the office next to Nathan's, and you'll be the liaison between the board and my office."

She rocked against the back of her chair in surprise. "Vice president? But I thought Milton Cranston was in line for that promotion. He's been here much longer than I have."

Jeff shook his head. "Milton's a good man, but he doesn't have your vivacious work ethic. Nathan thinks you can take this university to a higher level. And who knows, when I decide to retire, you may even take my place."

Danielle stood up and rubbed her forehead. "This is all happening too quickly. I had no idea."

He laughed. "Of course not, but that's what we've been planning."

"Of course I'm flattered…" His first statement flashed into her mind, and she hesitated. "Jeff, what did you mean when you said you didn't want me to do anything to jeopardize my work here?"

His face flushed, and he got up from his chair. "I'm going to be honest with you, Danielle. Nathan and I were both surprised to see you with that policeman at Nathan's on Saturday."

"*That policeman?* What do you mean?"

He came around the desk and faced her. "I know your personal life is your own, but we have high standards for our faculty here at Webster. Detective Denton is a little too rough around the edges to fit in with your friends. Besides, with your new position, you'll probably be making three or four times his salary."

Danielle frowned. "Money isn't the most important thing in life, Jeff. People and relationships come before that. I've always believed that."

"I know you do, but you need to think about impressions, too. As vice president of the school you will deal with the donors, and we have some of the richest people in the country on our list. I hardly think Jack Denton fits into their world."

Danielle took a step back from Jeff and shook her head. "Have you forgotten where I come from? My parents struggled to make their living in one of the toughest industries in the nation. They always told me they considered everybody they worked with important to their music, even to the custodian who swept up the studio after they were through recording. That's the way I feel, Jeff. I don't see differences in people and where they fall on somebody else's idea of a social scale."

Jeff spread his hands in a pleading manner. "Danielle, we just want to help you."

"We?" Her body straightened. "Does Nathan feel the same way?"

Jeff nodded. "Yes. You have a great future here, and we want you to achieve it."

Jack had been right. Nathan and Jeff had made him feel like he didn't fit into her world. She'd been oblivious to his feelings, and their friendship had ended. In her heart she knew something else—she would never feel about Webster University the same again.

She'd held such hopes for how this school was preparing her for life when she'd come as a freshman. Now she saw it as something entirely different. She could never think of Webster again without thinking of Jennifer's and Tricia's deaths. Now she would have to add Jack Denton and what might have been to that list.

Danielle squared her shoulders. "Thank you for wanting to help me, Jeff. I think you have."

He smiled. "That's wonderful. I knew you'd see it our way."

She tilted her head and regarded the man she'd respected for years. "No, I don't think I'll ever see it your way. A long time ago my parents taught me that God loves me in spite of all my faults, and because of that I have to show love and respect to everyone around me. I don't see class distinctions the way you and Nathan do."

He cocked an eyebrow and directed a skeptical grin toward her. "Come now, Danielle. You can't make me believe that you see the janitors and cooks at this school as important as those of us who educate the students."

"Oh, but I do, Jeff. They may not have had the opportunities I've had, but that doesn't change the fact we're all God's children."

He waved his hand in dismissal. "Well, after you become vice president, you can treat them any way you want."

The picture her father had shown her of a Batwa man flashed into her mind, and she shook her head. "I don't think I'll be doing that because I don't plan to take the job."

His mouth gaped open. "What?"

She smiled. "No, I've been thinking about leaving Webster for quite some time. After the first of the year I'm going to work with my parents in their ministry to the Batwa people in Africa. I'll have my resignation on your desk in the next few days. I'm sure you can find somebody else to take my place here."

Before he had time to respond, she whirled and strode from the office. Betty looked up at her, but Danielle didn't stop. She could hardly wait to get to her office and call her parents. The decision she'd weighed for so many weeks had been made clear, and she realized God had chosen the right moment to reveal the answer. Webster held no future for her, but her parents' ministry did.

She closed her office door behind her and sank down in the chair behind her desk. The rose still lay where she'd left it. She picked it up and smelled the fragrance of the petals. The sweet odor couldn't cover up the smell of evil that she'd come to equate with Webster. Whoever was sending her these roses could be a part of it, too.

Grasping the bloom with one hand, she pulled the petals from the stem and threw them in the trash can. Then she dumped the stem and the card in with them. If someone had become interested in her, he needed to let her know, not play a silly game.

She stared into the can, and her heart pumped at what she'd just done. She picked up the phone to call her parents and glanced around the room. The office had become her second home over the past three years, but it would soon become a part of her past.

Tears formed in her eyes. She'd first met Jack in this room, and they'd talked here many times since. Regret filled her at the thought that leaving Webster also meant leaving him. She wondered how he would feel when he heard she was taking the job with the ministry. He, too, would soon be relegated to an interval in her past, and the thought made her sad.

The feeling she'd tried to ignore wouldn't be suppressed any longer. Jack Denton had become special to her. She shook her head—more than special. For all the good it did her, she'd succumbed to what she said she'd never do. She'd fallen for Jack, but he'd made it clear he didn't feel the same.

Tears slid down her cheeks. She crossed her arms on her desk and laid her head on them. In the end what she'd feared most had happened—she'd lost somebody else she loved.

Jack stared at the phone on his desk. He'd almost called Danielle over the weekend, even gone as far as dialing half her number before he hung up. What good would it do him? He'd just be prolonging the inevitable anyway. She had her life, and he didn't want to mess it up like he had for his wife.

He raked his hand through his hair and stood up. He needed something to distract him.

The door opened and Will walked in. "Morning, partner."

"Morning." Jack reached for the file he'd put together after talking to Landon Morse. "I think we need to follow up on this girl that Landon Morse was accused of stalking."

"Good idea. Do you have telephone numbers?"

"The girl lives in Thomasville, Texas, and Landon taught at a small college in Austin. I thought I'd call the Thomasville Police first and see what they can tell me before I contact the girl or her family."

Will motioned toward the phone. "Go on. I want to hear what they say."

Jack punched the number into the phone and waited. A woman answered. "Good morning. Thomasville Police Department. May I help you?"

Jack cleared his throat. "This is Detective Jack Denton with the Webster Falls, North Carolina, Sheriff's Department. I'd like to talk with the detective who investigated a case about four years ago involving the stalking of a young woman named Julie Travis."

"Would you hold please, and I'll try to locate one of our investigators."

Jack drummed his fingers on the desktop while he waited. Within minutes a male voice came on the line. "This is Detective Todd Clark. You say you want to know something about the Julie Travis case?"

Jack sat up straight. "Yes. We're investigating a murder in Webster Falls, and one of our suspects has a link to the case."

Detective Clark sighed. "I remember that case. Julie Travis accused her college professor of stalking her. She took one of his classes and had some trouble with the work. When she went to his office hours for extra help, he hit on her and she left. After that she said everywhere she went he showed up and watched her."

"That college professor was Landon Morse, and he teaches at a college here in Webster Falls. One of the students, a girl, was murdered a few weeks ago."

"Oh, man. I always thought he was a nut, but I couldn't prove anything. Their stories didn't match."

"Yeah, Morse has told me his side."

"Well, don't let that influence you," Detective Clark said. "The Austin police and our department both worked on that case. Just because we couldn't prove he stalked her doesn't mean it didn't happen. I talked to that girl and her family. She was scared to death."

"So what did you really think?"

Detective Clark hesitated. "Like I said I couldn't prove anything, but I believed the girl. She had her facts together, times and places where he showed up. All he did was deny it and talk about how she invited him to her apartment. She said that wasn't true, and I never could find anyone in her building who'd seen him visiting there."

"What did you do?"

"I helped her get an order of protection and told her if he bothered her again to let me know. He violated it once and spent a few days in jail. I never saw him again after that."

Jack picked up a pencil lying on his desk and pulled his notebook closer. "Spent a few days in jail, huh? Do you know how I could contact Julie Travis? I'd like to talk to her myself."

"Yeah, I know where you can locate her, but it won't do any good."

Jack's eyebrows arched. "You don't think she'd want to talk to me?"

"It's not that. She can't talk to you."

"Why?"

Detective Clark sighed. "A few days after Morse got out of jail, Julie was in an automobile accident that left her in a coma. Her parents kept her at home for a while, but they finally had to put her in a nursing home. I went by to see her once, and it tore me up seeing that beautiful girl lying there just shriveling up and dying."

A lump formed in Jack's throat, and he swallowed. "Do you think he had anything to do with the wreck?"

"I don't know. It happened on a deserted stretch of highway at night. She ran off the road and hit a tree. I figured Morse had to be involved, probably ran her off the road, but there wasn't any evidence to support it and Julie couldn't tell us what had happened. Since it was a state road, the highway patrol investigated and ruled it an accident. It wasn't taken any further."

Jack dropped the pencil to his desk and rubbed his hand across his eyes. "Well, thank you for your help. I'll let you know if we end up charging Morse with anything."

"Do that. I'd sure like to see him get what's coming to him."

Jack hung up and sank back in his chair. After re-capping the conversation to Will, he pushed back from his desk. "So now we know more about Landon Morse's past, but the girl who might be able to tell us about him is in a coma."

Will shook his head. "If that guy ran her off the road, then he's also capable of killing Tricia Peterson."

Jack nodded. "And don't forget he was here when Jennifer McCaslin was killed, too."

Will gave a low whistle. "Man, he's looking good for a suspect. We've just gotta figure out how to catch him."

As Will talked, Jack became aware of the tension in his body. Pains like small electrical charges shot up his back into his head. He stood, stretched his arms over his head and clasped his hands together. He pulled and twisted until the kinks in his back loosened. This case had him tied up in knots, and he needed to solve it.

The thought came to him that it might not be the case that had him out of sorts. It could be a woman who'd made him want to live again. That situation had about as much chance of working out as Julie Travis had of regaining consciousness. Both appeared hopeless.

FOURTEEN

On the way back from lunch, Danielle rounded the corner to her office and blinked in surprise at April standing outside the door in the hallway. The girl straightened from leaning against the wall when Danielle approached.

"There you are, Dr. Tyler. I wondered if you were out of the office this afternoon."

Puzzled, Danielle shook her head. "No, but why are you out here? Anytime you get here before me you can go in and begin work."

April followed Danielle into the office and headed to her desk. "I know, but I didn't want to come in alone. I didn't mind waiting."

Danielle studied April as she walked to her computer and turned it on. Her mood wasn't as perky as usual, and her eyes looked tired.

"April, is something wrong?"

She leaned over to pull something from the bottom drawer of the desk. "I'm okay."

Danielle frowned at the quiet tone of the girl's voice. "You're not yourself. Tell me what's bothering you."

April straightened in her chair, and Danielle's eyebrows arched at the fear she saw in the girl's eyes. As if an internal faucet had been turned on, tears flowed down her face. "Oh, Dr. Tyler," she cried, "I'm so scared."

Danielle rushed past the desk and put her arms around April's shaking shoulders. "Tell me what's happened."

April pulled a tissue from her pocket and wiped her eyes. "For several weeks I've been getting these anonymous messages. At first I thought they were a joke, like one of my friends was trying to creep me out, but they've all sworn they didn't send them."

The skin on the back of Danielle's neck prickled as if an icy hand had clamped down on her. "Did they come in the mail?"

April shook her head. "Not through the postal service, but through campus mail."

"So that's why you thought they were being sent by a friend."

"Yes. There was no return address. Just my name and campus box number written on the envelope. I asked the man who runs our post office if there was any way to trace where it came from, and he said no. Since their service doesn't require postage for anything delivered on campus, students and faculty can send each other mail by just dropping it in the box."

Danielle stood up and peered down at April. "What did the messages say?"

"Oh, they'd mention how good I looked that day and describe what I was wearing and where I was at a certain time. I knew it had to be a guy by the way he described the way I looked. Then they got worse."

"How?"

April twisted the tissue between her fingers. "He said when I least expected to see him, he'd be there. That we were meant to be together, and he could make me happier than any of the guys I'd dated before."

Chills ran up Danielle's spine. "Do you think you've been followed by anyone?"

April nodded. "I went to the library Friday night, and when I was going back to my room, I thought I saw a man in the trees by the dorm. I ran inside and peeked out the door, but he'd gone. Then last night I came back from eating dinner with friends. When I walked from my car to the dorm, I heard footsteps behind me."

Danielle walked back to her desk, dropped down in her chair and reached for the phone. "I don't like the sound of this. We've got to call the police."

April's tears flowed again. "I wanted to call them, but I was afraid they'd say I was paranoid and that they couldn't do anything for me."

"They won't think that. They're here to protect citizens."

April's eyes grew wide, and a smile creased her lips. "Are you going to call that good-looking detective who questioned me?"

Danielle sighed in exasperation. "April, it doesn't matter who comes. I want you to back off your flirting. That may be what got you in this mess to start with. You have a reputation on campus as a girl aggressive with the opposite sex. Somebody may be trying to scare you because you've teased the wrong person."

April's face paled, and she clamped her lips together. She didn't say anything but nodded. With a sigh Danielle picked up the phone. She knew the number she had to dial, but she hesitated. What if Jack thought she was using this situation as a ploy to get him back to her office?

One look at April's face told her it didn't matter what Jack thought. She had a responsibility to the students at Webster, and she wouldn't back away even if it meant she had to endure Jack's presence.

She breathed a quick prayer for strength to talk to him again and dialed the number.

Jack sipped a cup of coffee as he looked over the notes he'd made while talking to the detective on the Julie Travis case. Although he'd never seen the girl, he felt sympathy for her and her family. They were like so many others he'd known, shattered by tragedy in their lives.

He couldn't help but wonder if Landon Morse had anything to do with her accident. Maybe he should call the man in and talk with him again about the circumstances surrounding the dismissal from his job in Austin. And what about Jeff Newman and Nathan Webster? Had they knowingly hired a man suspected of stalking a student? If they had, they needed their heads examined. A teacher with a problem of stalking didn't need to be around female students.

The phone rang, and he reached across his desk. Without looking at the caller ID, he spoke into the receiver. "Jack Denton."

"Hello, Jack. This is Danielle."

He swallowed and straightened in his chair. He tried to respond, but the words wouldn't come. He pushed the notepad away, propped his elbow on the desk and rubbed his eyes. A vision of how she'd looked when she ran into her house on Saturday night returned, and his heart pounded.

"Danielle, how are you?"

"I'm fine, but I'm calling about April. She's in my office and needs to talk with you."

Jack groaned inwardly at the memory of the girl and the way she'd scooted her chair so close to his when he questioned her. "What is it this time, Danielle?"

The door opened and Will, his attention directed to a sheet of paper in his hand, ambled in. "I wanted to check with you…" He hesitated and took a step backward when he saw Jack on the phone. "Sorry," he whispered, "I didn't know you were on the phone."

"Hold on a minute, Danielle," Jack said. He covered the phone's mouthpiece with his hand and motioned for Will to come on in. "Danielle says one of her students needs to talk to us. I may ask you to go out to the school with me." He grasped the receiver tighter, clenched his jaw and removed his hand from the mouthpiece. "Now what is it that April wants to report?"

He listened as Danielle told him about the anonymous messages and April's suspicions that she was being followed. As Danielle spoke, he tried to concentrate on her words but found himself thinking about how sad she'd looked on the ride back from Nathan's house on Saturday night.

When she mentioned the suspected stalker, Jack sat up straight in his chair and glanced down at the notes he'd made when speaking to the detective in Thomasville. If Landon Morse had stalked Julie Travis, he might be doing the same to April. This could be the break he'd been waiting for in this case.

"So," Danielle said, "I really think you need to talk with April. She's terrified, and I believe her."

Jack nodded. "Will and I can be there in fifteen

minutes. Have her stay in your office, and we'll talk to her there."

"I will, Jack, and thank you."

"Thank you for calling. See you in a few minutes."

Tiny shivers ran up his arm as he replaced the receiver in the handset. He knew it came from the pleasure he got in hearing her soft voice. He wondered how she looked this morning, if her weekend had been as unsettling as his. He'd rattled around his apartment all day Sunday trying to forget how abrupt he'd been with her after they left the party. He needed to apologize for that, but she might take it as a signal he wanted to see her again.

He did want to see her again, to sit with her and feel the peace he had just listening to her talk. He shook the thought from his head. There was no going back now. She probably hated him after the way he'd spoken to her the last time they were together.

"Are you going to tell me what that was about, or are you just going to sit there all day thinking about it?"

Jack jerked his attention back to Will who sat down in the chair facing his desk. "Sorry. That was Danielle on the phone. Her student worker thinks she's being stalked. We need to go out to the school and talk with her."

Will jumped up from the chair. "Then let's go. Maybe we'll get a lead in the murder case."

Jack stood, walked to the coatrack beside the door, and pulled his jacket from one of the hooks. Slipping it on, he opened the door. "Come on. You drive."

Jack strode down the hall toward the parking lot with Will behind. With each step he grew more excited. Once outside, he increased his gait until he reached Will's car. He reached out to open the door and glanced over his shoulder at Will, who was just rounding the back of the car.

Will glared at him over the top of the car. "Remind me not to challenge you to a foot race. I might have a heart attack trying to beat you."

Jack chuckled. "Just eager to question this girl, Will."

Will opened the door and laughed. "You can't fool me. It isn't the student you want to see."

Jack's face warmed, and he climbed in the car. Closing the door, he reached for his seat belt and buckled it. "You're really funny, Will. Just drive. Okay?"

As the car pulled out of the parking lot, Jack turned his head and stared out the window. He wondered if his excitement to see Danielle again was evident. If so, he'd have to guard his behavior around Danielle today.

It didn't matter what he felt. Danielle deserved more from someone than what he could offer. Now everything would be fine if he could just keep that in mind when he saw her again.

* * *

When the soft knock tapped on the door, Danielle swallowed her apprehension at seeing Jack again and put her hand on April's arm. "I'll get it."

As if she moved in slow motion, Danielle crept across the floor. She'd hoped to have more time before seeing Jack again. Now with him here, she had to mask any feelings she might have and concentrate on April's dilemma.

Her heart pumped as she opened the door for them to enter her office. "Come in. I'm glad you could come."

Jack nodded, the remoteness in his eyes chilling her. "Will and I are very interested in what April has to tell us."

Danielle smiled at the detective she'd met the day after Tricia's murder. "Hello, Detective Bryson. It's good to see you again."

He smiled, and the dimples in his cheeks winked at her. "Thank you, Dr. Tyler. I'm surprised you remember my name. We had such a brief meeting."

His easy manner relaxed her. "Jack has told me a lot about you. He really values you as his partner."

Will's eyebrows arched, and he punched Jack on the shoulder. "You'd never know it from the way he treats me." He grinned at her. "He's a tough cookie. Not one to give out many compliments."

Danielle wanted to say that Jack had a side he kept

hidden from most people, but the glare he directed at Will changed her mind. "Detective Bryson, this is April Brockwell. Jack is already acquainted with her."

Will slipped past Danielle and walked toward April with his hand extended. "Miss Brockwell, I'm Detective Bryson. We're here to question you about the problem you're having."

Danielle glanced back at Will and April, who sat down facing each other just as April and Jack had done days before. She took a deep breath. "I think I'll go get a cup of coffee while you two talk to April."

She turned to go, but Jack reached out and touched her arm. "Don't say anything to anyone about us being here. We need to keep this quiet."

When he released her, the skin where his fingers had been tingled. "I'll be in the dining room if you need me."

She whirled and rushed out the door before he could say anything. In the hallway she sagged against the wall and rubbed her arm where his hand had been moments before.

After several minutes she straightened and gritted her teeth. She had to quit thinking about Jack Denton. He'd been honest with her from the beginning about his determination not to repeat old mistakes by becoming involved with a woman. No matter what her feelings had become, she was better off without him.

All she needed to do was get through the next few

weeks and she could leave Webster University and Jack Denton behind. There were far more important matters waiting to occupy her mind, and she could hardly wait to let them replace the empty feeling she had every time she thought about Jack.

and the words were so densely impacted and illegible penned in a larger, messier hand than they're writing. Jumping out anon are enlightment rarely drawn at a distance the manuscript the hundred and.

FIFTEEN

Thirty minutes later Danielle stood outside her closed office door. She'd thought Jack and Will would be finished by now, but no one had come out since she'd returned from the dining room. What could be taking them so long?

The door opened, and Will walked into the hallway. He grinned when he saw her. "What are you doing out here? Come on in. It's your office."

"I didn't want to disturb."

His dimples creased his cheeks. "Do you mean Jack?" He leaned closer and whispered. "I think you disturb him every time he gets around you."

"I would think you'd be a better detective than that." Danielle's face burned, and she pushed past Will.

Inside the room, April sat at her desk, her hands clasped in her lap. Jack stood at the window gazing across the campus. Danielle stopped beside her desk, unsure what she should do.

Will ambled up beside her as Jack turned around. "Is everything okay?" Danielle asked.

Jack nodded. "April has told us what's been going on for the past few weeks. We need to catch this guy, and April has agreed to help us."

Danielle glanced from Jack to April. "How are you going to do that?"

Fear etched April's face. "They want to see if he'll follow a decoy."

Danielle turned to Will. "I don't understand."

"I've been on the phone with the sheriff, and we have the details worked out. Our department has a female deputy who is about April's size. When April goes to the library tonight, we'll be waiting inside. She's going to wear a hooded coat, and Deputy Riley will put it on and take her books. Then our deputy will walk across campus toward the dorm. If the guy is watching, maybe he'll follow the decoy, and we'll have a chance to get him."

Danielle glanced toward Jack. "What if he doesn't appear?"

Jack shrugged. "We'll try another night. It's a long shot, but this could be a break in Tricia's murder."

Danielle turned toward the door. "I need to tell Jeff and Nathan about this."

Will grabbed her arm. "No, Dr. Tyler. The fewer people who know about this the better. We don't know who this guy is, and we don't want him to find out we're watching."

She looked at Jack, and he nodded his agreement. She started to offer a further argument but knew it would do no good. "I understand. Is there any way I can help?"

April stood up. "Could you be at the library waiting for me? I'd feel better if you were there."

"Of course. Anything else?"

Jack stepped away from the window. "Can you arrange a private room at the library where I can wait with Deputy Riley until April gets there?"

Danielle nodded. "I'll tell the staff I need the conference room on the second floor for a meeting tonight. You can stay there."

The muscle in Jack's jaw twitched. "That sounds good." He turned back to April. "Now be sure and wear a hooded coat and carry several books. Don't hurry when you walk across campus. Act like you have all the time in the world. The sheriff is making arrangements with the university security service to have some officers join our deputies on the stakeout. They'll be watching every move you make. When you get to the library, go to one of the study tables and sit down. You need to pretend to study for about an hour."

A groan rumbled in April's throat. "I don't know if I can do that."

"Yes, you can," Jack insisted. "Whoever is following you may come inside to make sure you're studying. We want him to see you. After about an hour get up and come to the conference room. Deputy Riley will take your place and walk back to the dorm. If anybody's out there, we'll see him."

April buried her head in her hands. "I just want this to be over." After a moment she uncovered her face and turned to Danielle. "I've thought a lot about what you said today, Dr. Tyler. If we catch this guy, I'm going to be more careful in the future."

Danielle put her arm around April's shoulders. "You're a smart and beautiful young woman. You just need to make sure everybody sees you for what you really are, not the tease that you try to be at times."

April's lips trembled, and she grasped Danielle's hand. "Thank you for being so nice to me." She glanced at Will and then Jack. "And thank you both for trying to help me."

Will smiled. "Happy to do it. Maybe we'll catch this creep tonight, and your troubles will be over."

"I hope so." She wiped her eyes and took a deep breath. "Now if you don't need me anymore, I have a class."

Jack waved his hand in dismissal. "Go on. We'll see you in the conference room tonight. Get to the library about eight o'clock, and then come to the conference room about nine."

April nodded. "I'll see you then."

Will walked April to the door, then turned to Jack. "I'm going on out to the car, Jack. I need to make some phone calls. Come on whenever you're ready." He smiled at Danielle. "It was good to see you again, Dr. Tyler."

"You, too, Detective Bryson. I suppose I'll see you at the library tonight." When he'd disappeared out the door, she faced Jack. "Do you think he'll show?"

Jack shrugged. "I don't know. Sometimes we have luck on the first try, and sometimes we never get the guy."

She crossed her arms and hugged her body. "I'm beginning to think that this campus spawns evil at every turn. Two students murdered and now another being stalked. When is it ever going to end?"

Jack shook his head. "I don't know. Maybe soon if this stalker is connected to the killings."

Danielle straightened and gritted her teeth. "Well, it won't be too soon for me. I'm beginning to hate the place. I should have known better than to come back here. It's not only brought back my nightmares about Jennifer, but now Tricia's murder haunts me, too. Maybe it's best that I'm leaving."

Jack's eyebrows arched. "Leaving? What do you mean?"

"I've decided to take the job with my parents." Danielle searched his face for a hint that he wanted her to stay, but she saw nothing.

His mouth thinned into a straight line. "I see. When did you decide?"

"This morning when Jeff offered me the job as vice president. It seems he and Nathan have been grooming me for that position."

His gaze flitted across her face, and her skin prickled at his intense stare. "Why don't you want the job? I think you'd be great at it."

She reached out and grabbed the back of a chair to steady her trembling legs. The breath had left her body as if someone had punched a hole in her chest, and a weakness flowed from her head to her toes. Why couldn't he say he didn't want her to go?

Danielle blinked back tears and took a deep breath. "I'm sure I could do it, but there's another faculty member who deserves it more than I do. All I want is to feel safe again." Her gaze raked the walls of her office. "There's nothing safe about this place anymore. I want to be with my parents and try to find my life again. Maybe I can do that by joining their new ministry."

He nodded. "I hope you'll be happy, Danielle." He reached for his ever-present notebook he'd set on her desk and picked it up. "Well, I'd better get out of here. I'll see you at the library tonight."

"I'll be there."

She followed him to the door and closed it when he stepped into the hall. She leaned her forehead against the wood and let the tears trickle down her cheeks. She wanted to tell him that she had something new from Webster to add to her list of things that haunted her. He now occupied a spot, and she doubted if she would ever be able to erase his name from her heart.

The sad thing, however, was that he didn't appear to care she was leaving. He had reacted as if she were some casual acquaintance that he could care less whether or not they ever met again. For Danielle that wasn't the case.

She still didn't know when it had happened. At some point when she'd let her guard down, Jack Denton had wedged his way into her heart, and no amount of wishing would make him go away.

Jack paced back and forth across the conference room but stopped every few minutes to check his watch. Deputy Ann Riley sat at the long table that stretched nearly the full length of the room and flipped through a magazine she'd found in one of the chairs.

She glanced up as Jack made another sweep across the small room. "Why don't you sit down? You're making me antsy."

He shook his head. "I can't. I always get this way during a stakeout."

She turned another page and bent over to study a picture. "I'm the one who's going to be in danger if anything goes wrong, and I'm not worried. You just need to relax."

He dropped down in a chair across from her and rubbed the back of his neck. As he studied the deputy, he was amazed how much she resembled April. About the same height and weight, the only difference was Ann's blond hair, but that would be covered by the hood. "We're not going to let anything happen to you. We have men stationed all across campus. As soon as you leave here, they'll have you on their radar. They'll make sure nothing happens to you."

She flipped the magazine closed and chuckled. "I know, Jack. I'm not worried. I'm wired, and I'll be in voice contact with all of you every step of the way." She pushed back from the table. "In fact I feel kind of pumped. I sure hope we can bring this guy down."

"Me, too."

Ann stretched her arms over her head and twisted at the waist from side to side. "I need to stretch some before I go out there, though. I'd sure hate to be taken by surprise."

Jack pushed up from his chair and walked around the table. He swallowed back the fear that rose in his throat. "Don't worry, Ann. We'll make sure that doesn't happen."

Her eyes narrowed, and for an instant Jack spotted what he thought might be uncertainty. He understood her concern. No matter how many precautions they took, something could always go wrong when you were dealing with an unstable person. To his way of thinking anyone who would terrorize another person had to be a nutcase.

Before he could respond to Ann, the door opened and Danielle walked in. His heart kicked him in the chest at the sight of her. She'd never looked more beautiful with her nose and cheeks red from the outside cold.

"I've been in my office, but April just called. She's on her way to the library. So I came on over."

Jack glanced at Ann. "This is Dr. Danielle Tyler. She's the Dean of Students here." He directed his attention back to Danielle. "This is Deputy Ann Riley. She's going to be our decoy tonight."

Danielle pulled off her gloves and extended her hand to Ann. "It's so nice to meet you, Deputy Riley. I can't tell you how much I appreciate what you're doing to help April. I'm really concerned about her."

Ann shook Danielle's hand and smiled. "It's good to meet you, too, Dr. Tyler. I hope we can put an end to this business tonight."

Danielle sighed. "I do, too, but please call me Danielle."

Ann pulled out a chair and motioned for Danielle to sit down. "I will, and you call me Ann. I feel I know you already, because Jack has told me about your link to the murders here at Webster."

"I've lived a nightmare for years."

Jack detected the tremor in her voice, and it was all he could do to keep from sitting in the chair beside her and grasping her hand. Instead he turned his back and headed for the door. If this stakeout proved successful, they might be able to answer the question of who had committed the murders that haunted Danielle.

"I think I'll see if April's here yet," he said as he opened the door. "I'll be back when she comes up here."

He slipped into the hall and looked around for a place where he could stand and be unobserved by people coming and going from the library. A waist-high wall with a railing on top covered the length of the second floor and provided a bird's-eye view of the main floor of the library below. Long shelves of books known as the stacks ran parallel to the wall from the front of the second floor to the back.

Jack stepped behind the first row of the stacks and pulled several books from the shelf. He peered through the hole he'd made to the lower level of the building. From his vantage point he could see the study tables and chairs that dotted the main floor. This spot seemed the perfect place to watch without being observed.

He'd only been there a few minutes when April walked into the library. She wore a hooded coat just as he'd told her and carried a large three-ring binder with two books perched atop. She glanced at the tables before she settled at an unoccupied one, pulled her coat off, and opened one of the books. Within minutes she appeared to be engrossed in one of the books she'd brought as she read and made notes.

He unclipped the radio from his belt and gave the prearranged signal that April had entered the library. "The package has arrived."

"Ten-four." Will's reply confirmed his stakeout position.

Before he could respond, the front door opened again, and Jeff Newman walked into the library. He stopped just inside and glanced around at the students scattered at the tables before he walked to the circulation desk.

"We have a visitor."

The student worker smiled as Jeff approached. Jack tensed and tried to hear what they were saying, but he was too far away. He'd forgotten how quiet it was in a library. The silence settled over him and sent an icy foreboding flowing through him.

The student worker pulled a book from underneath the circulation desk. Smiling, Jeff took it, shook the young man's hand and walked from the room.

"School president on his way out. See where he goes."

"Ten-four."

Within minutes the voice of one of the deputies stationed across campus came over the radio. "He's gone inside the Administration Building. I just saw the light in a downstairs office go on."

"Keep a watch," Jack said.

He stared back at April, who hadn't moved and seemed more involved in her studies than before. The door opened again, and Jack's eyebrows arched as Landon Morse walked in. "What have we here?"

Will said, "I just saw him arrive. Let us know if he leaves."

"Ten-four."

Landon ambled to a reading area at the back of the downstairs. He studied the newspapers on a table before he picked one up, sat down in a chair and crossed his legs. Opening up the paper, he held it in front of his face. From time to time he lowered the paper to turn the page and direct a stare in April's direction. Jack cautioned himself about making too many assumptions, but Landon appeared to be watching April.

For the next hour Jack watched from his hiding place. A little after nine, April stood, closed her books and walked to the circulation desk. She spoke to the worker there for a moment and nodded as he pointed toward the stacks upstairs.

"Good girl," Jack breathed. So far she had followed their instructions. Now she had to convince anyone watching that she was going to the stacks to find a book. This would be the ploy to get her to the conference room and for Ann to take her place.

Landon stood up, folded the newspaper and placed it back on the table. As April mounted the stairs that led to the second level, Landon walked from the building. Was it a coincidence, Jack wondered, or was Landon getting ready to follow her when she left? And what about Jeff Newman? Could he have slipped from his office and be waiting somewhere on campus?

Jack shook his head. For all they knew the stalker could be someone they'd never encountered. If they were lucky, tonight might answer a lot of questions.

SIXTEEN

Ann pushed up from her chair as Jack slipped into the conference room. "Is it time?"

He nodded. "April's on her way up now."

The door opened, and April entered the room. Her hands shook as she laid the books and binder on the table. She tossed her hooded coat on one of the chairs and turned to Jack. "Were you watching? How did I do?"

He smiled. "I was hidden in the stacks and could see you from the time you entered. You did exactly what we'd asked you to do. Now we'll see if anyone took the bait."

Danielle moved around the table and put her arm around the girl's shoulders. "I know this wasn't easy, April, but maybe it'll be over before long."

Ann picked up the coat, shrugged into it and looped the buttons into their holes. She ran her hands down the front and smiled. "Perfect fit. I thought we were about the same size."

Jack pointed to the hood. "Be sure and pull that up around your face. When you leave the building, hold the books close to your chest and tuck your chin down. We don't want your face to be visible."

Ann laughed. "You sound like I've never done this before."

Danielle reached out and grasped Ann's arm. Her forehead wrinkled, and concern lined her face. "Be careful, Ann."

She patted Danielle's hand. "Don't worry. This is just part of my job. Besides, I'm wired to everybody. So I'll probably be talking to them all the way across campus." She took a deep breath and glanced at Jack. "Whenever you're ready, I am, too."

Jack nodded. "I'm going out the back way. Give me time to get in place. Then you leave through the front door and walk toward the dorm. The minute you spot anyone, let us know, and we'll close in."

"Will do." Ann took a deep breath and picked up the books.

Jack turned toward the door, but Danielle stepped in front of him before he could get there. "What should April and I do?"

He stared down into her eyes. "Stay here. April doesn't need to be seen by anyone until this thing's over. If something happens, I'll let you know."

Before she could question him further, he eased from the room. He headed to the stairs at the back of the second level and descended. Exiting the library by a side door, he slipped into the shadows covering the Webster University campus.

Security lights burned in the buildings that loomed around the secluded quadrangle that lay within the campus. On most of his visits here he'd seen students strolling down the paths that crisscrossed the area or lounging underneath the huge oaks scattered across the landscape. Tonight the campus appeared deserted.

It only took a few seconds to find his assigned post behind a tree outside the library. Once he was settled, he pulled the radio to his mouth. "It's showtime."

He could imagine the officers stationed in the darkness as they came to attention and waited for what was about to happen. As if on cue, Ann walked out of the library and began her journey into the night.

Her face wasn't visible, and he breathed a sigh of relief. A gust of wind blew down from the surrounding mountain, and her coat fluttered about her legs. She clutched the books closer and bent her head toward them. He watched as she passed his point and proceeded in the direction of the dorms.

"Anything yet?" he heard her say.

"Negative," someone responded.

She passed the stakeout positions of two more officers and received the same response. Jack fought the urge to leave his spot and trail her. He leaned against the tree and willed himself to stay put.

"I hear footsteps. Someone's behind me."

Jack jerked erect at the sound of Ann's voice. "Slow down," Jack whispered. "See if he'll approach you."

"There's a parking lot to the side of the dorm. It looks dark because some of the lights aren't burning. I think I'll head there."

"Be careful, Ann. We don't know what this guy might do."

"I will. I'm stepping into the parking lot now. On my way toward the back." She paused, then spoke in an excited voice. "Here he comes."

The sound of a collision echoed in Jack's ear, and a groan as if the air had been knocked from someone's body followed. Jack bolted from his hiding place. "All units to the dorm parking lot."

As he ran, officers and university security personnel converged from their positions across the campus. Jack sprinted forward, his chest heaving. Just before he reached the parking lot, Will appeared beside him.

They jumped the curb and bolted between the parked cars to the back of the lot. They stopped in surprise at the sight before them. Landon Morse lay facedown on the ground, his hands cuffed behind him. Ann Riley stood over him, her gun drawn and aimed at the man's back.

"One false move, and it'll be your last."

Will stopped beside Ann. "Are you all right?"

She grinned. "Yeah. I'll probably be a little sore in

the morning from this guy jumping on my back. Too bad nobody told him I'm the judo instructor for all the policemen in this area."

"Yeah, too bad," Jack said, and grabbed the man's shoulders. "Okay, on your feet, Morse."

Landon wobbled as Jack propelled him upward. Once on his feet, he straightened to his full height and glared at Jack. "What's the meaning of this? I was on the way to my car when this crazy woman attacked me."

"Save it for the judge, Morse. You're under arrest for stalking a female and attacking a police officer," Jack said. He turned back to Ann. "Do you want to read him his rights? I need to get back to the library and tell them what's happened. I'll bring April and Danielle to the station."

Ann nodded. "It'll be my pleasure, Detective Denton." She faced Landon. "You have the right…"

Her words faded as Jack jogged back to the library. He wanted April to know that her stalker had been caught, but most of all he wanted to see Danielle. He hoped before morning came he would have the answers to questions that had plagued her for years.

April pushed up from her chair and walked to the door of the conference room. "How much longer do you think it'll take?"

Danielle smiled at the girl who'd asked the same

question every five minutes since Ann left. She rose and went to stand beside her. Taking April by the hand, she guided her back to her chair. "I don't know. Jack will let us know as soon as he can. In the meantime we have to be patient."

April sat back down and massaged her temples with her fingers. "I know, but this waiting is awful."

Danielle slumped into her chair and looked at her watch. Jack had been gone about twenty minutes. Surely it hadn't taken that long for Ann to make her way to the dorm. Uneasiness probed at her mind. She'd had enough time unless something had happened. Danielle wanted to know what was going on as much as April, but she had to keep the girl calm until word arrived.

"Like I said, we just have to be—"

The door opened, interrupting her. Jack strode into the room. A big smile covered his face. "Good news. Ann was attacked on her way to the dorm, and we've arrested the stalker."

Danielle sprang from her chair. She clutched at her throat. "Is Ann all right?"

Jack chuckled. "Yeah. Too bad I can't say the same thing for the poor guy. He didn't realize he was tangling with a judo instructor."

April, her face pale, rose slowly from her chair. "So you caught the person who's been sending me the notes and following me?"

Jack nodded. "It looks like we have. He's on his way to headquarters right now. How would you like to go down there?"

April glanced at Danielle. "Will you go with me, Dr. Tyler?"

Danielle put her arm around April's shoulder. "I'd be happy to go." She turned back to Jack. "Who is it? Do we know him?"

A slow smile spread across Jack's face as he glanced from one to the other. "You do. It was Landon Morse."

April's eyes grew wide, and her body tensed. "Dr. M-Morse?" April sputtered. "I'm in his music appreciation course. Why would he stalk me?"

Jack shrugged. "I don't know. Have you had any problems? Have you been to his office for help?"

April thought for a moment, her eyes narrowed. "Yes, I went early in the semester. We were studying the Baroque period, and I was having some problems identifying the music of some of the composers. I went once or twice during his office hours for some extra help. I remember looking up once, and he had a strange expression on his face. But then, most of the kids think he's weird."

In all the years she'd known Landon, Danielle had thought him strange, but she really didn't believe him to be capable of violence. Could she have been so wrong? "Do you think he's the one who's been sending me the roses?"

Jack's eyes bored into her. "I wish I could set your mind at ease, Danielle, but at the moment I don't know. I hope to find that out."

"And Jennifer and Tricia?"

"I'd only be speculating at this point." He pointed toward the door. "But let's not waste time talking. I need to get to the station." He pulled off the jacket he was wearing and handed it to April. "Wear this. It's cold out there, and we'll have to hold your coat as evidence."

April frowned. "Why?"

"Ann came out of the confrontation okay, but Landon didn't fare as well. There's some of his blood on the coat. We'll need to do a DNA test to prove he was the one who attacked Ann."

April shuddered. "Then you can keep it. I don't want it back if it has a speck of his blood on it." She pulled on Jack's coat and walked toward the door.

Jack looked at Danielle, and she tried to determine what he was feeling. Was he wondering as she was if Landon had committed the two murders, or was he simply glad to put an end to April's fear? How she wished he could end hers.

He pulled her coat from the back of a chair and held it open. "Ready to go?"

She turned her back and slipped her arms inside. He slid the coat over her shoulders. She didn't know if it was her imagination, but he seemed to linger a moment before he released his grasp. Her heart leaped, and she turned to stare up into his face.

His gaze raked her face, but there was nothing personal in his scrutiny. She saw only the remote Jack she'd encountered when they first met, and despair settled over her. She had to quit trying to see feelings that weren't there. The sooner she faced that, the better off she'd be.

Danielle swallowed the last of the cold coffee in the cup and tossed it in the waste can. She turned and looked at April, who sat hunched in a chair beside Jack's desk. They had been in his office for what seemed like an eternity. A glance at her watch confirmed that in reality two hours had passed since Jack had ushered them inside and disappeared to question Landon.

April shifted in her chair and sighed. "When are they going to let us know anything?"

Danielle bit back the retort that April had asked the same question every ten minutes. Settling into the chair behind Jack's desk, she crossed her arms on its top and leaned forward. "I don't know. I'm sure they'll let us know as soon as they can."

April stood and walked to the one window in the room. Wrapping her arms around her waist, she stared out into the night. "I still can't believe it was Professor Morse."

The memory returned of how she used to spot Landon wherever she went, and Danielle shivered. How could she have been so naive that she didn't realize he was following her, too? Would Jennifer still be alive if she'd been more observant then?

Danielle leaned back in Jack's chair, placed her hands on the chair's arms and caressed the wood. It felt warm to her touch, and she could imagine his fingers having rubbed the same area. With a grunt she slumped back into the chair. She had to quit thinking like that.

The door opened, and she sat upright. Jack, his face lined with fatigue, entered the room. April hurried from where she stood by the window and stopped next to him. "What did you find out?"

Jack glanced from Danielle to April and let out a long breath as he rubbed the back of his neck. "We're going to book Morse on the charges of stalking and assault with intent to do bodily harm."

April collapsed into the chair where she'd sat moments before and began to sob. Danielle rushed around the desk and knelt next to her. "It's okay, April. It's all over now." She hugged the girl before she pushed to her feet and faced Jack. "That's wonderful news. But what about Tricia? Did he confess to her murder?"

Jack shook his head. "He's confessed to stalking April and attacking Ann, but he won't budge on the killings. He vows he had nothing to do with Tricia's and Jennifer's murders. In fact he keeps asking us to do a polygraph to prove him innocent."

"Are you going to do it?"

"I don't know. It might not be admissible in court. So we'll see. But for now, he's behind bars and isn't going anywhere."

Another thought struck Danielle. "What about Jeff and Nathan? Do they know about this yet?"

Jack shrugged. "I don't know. Since you're with the university, I'll let you take care of that. Now if you'll excuse me, I need to get back. You two might as well leave." He glanced down at April, who still wiped at her tears. "You're not going to be needed now."

She stood and held out her hand. "Thank you, Detective Denton, for all you've done for me. Please thank Deputy Riley also. She put her life on the line for me tonight, and I'll never forget her for that."

The half smile Danielle knew so well pulled at Jack's lips. "We were all just doing our jobs. I'm glad it turned out okay for you."

He turned to leave, but Danielle grabbed his arm. "But what should I tell Nathan and Jeff about how long Landon will be in jail?"

Jack focused on her hand for a moment, and she released her hold. His shoulders drooped as he looked up at her. "Morse is facing some steep charges. If he's convicted, he could spend up to twenty years in jail.

He probably won't be back at Webster anytime soon. And, unless there are some new leads in the murders, I doubt if I will be, either."

His words were spoken in an ominous tone, but it was the grim line of his mouth that told Danielle this might be one of the last times she would be with Jack. She forced a smile to her lips. "I'll tell them. And thank you, Jack…" She hesitated for a moment. "For everything."

His gaze raked her face. "And you, too."

He whirled and strode from the office. She stared after him for a moment before she turned back to April. "Come on. Let's go. There's nothing else for us to do here."

April nodded and started for the door. She stopped and pulled off Jack's coat, which she still wore. "I forgot to give Detective Denton his jacket."

Danielle grasped the back and held it while April shrugged it from her shoulders. "I'll hang it on his chair," she said to April, who was already stepping into the hallway.

Danielle pressed the jacket to her chest as she stopped behind Jack's chair. Slowly she raised the coat to her nose and inhaled. The smell of his aftershave drifted up, and her heart thudded like a bass drum. She tucked the scent away in a corner of her mind for a memory, hung the jacket on the back of the chair and straightened her shoulders.

Jack was one more loss she would mourn, but there wasn't time for that now. She had to inform Jeff and Nathan about Landon's arrest and see what the school's response to this scandal would be.

SEVENTEEN

Jack stumbled into the kitchen and groaned when he saw the remains of yesterday's coffee still in the pot. Muttering under his breath about how he had to do better with his housekeeping chores, he washed the pot, spooned fresh coffee into the filter and poured water into the tank.

He dropped into a chair at the kitchen table and glanced at the clock on the wall above the sink—8:00 a.m. He'd been at the station all night and had just come home to shower and have a cup of coffee before returning for another full day of duty. He hooked his foot in the chair next to him and pulled it away from the table far enough to prop his feet on the seat.

The steady rhythm of the dripping coffee relaxed him, and his eyes drooped. In his mind he could see Danielle as she looked last night when she thanked him. He'd wanted to grasp her shoulders and pull her to him, but he'd known better. He wondered what she'd meant when she added "for everything" as if it were an afterthought.

He nodded and drifted on the edge of sleep. His cell phone rang, and he jerked upright, almost turning over backward in his chair. He grabbed for the edge of the table with one hand and steadied himself while pulling the phone from his pocket with the other.

"Hello."

"Jack, this is Danielle. How are you this morning?"

Her voice drifted into his ear like the sweetest music he'd ever heard. "I'm fine."

"Did you get to go home last night?"

"No, I just got here a few minutes ago. I'm going to shower, then it's back to work."

"I'm sorry, but I suppose that's the life of a policeman."

"Yeah, it is."

"I'm already at school and getting ready to meet with Jeff and Nathan."

"I see."

His fingers tightened on the phone. Why was she calling him? He waited for her to continue.

She cleared her throat. "Uh, I suppose you wonder why I'm calling, especially after the way we parted on Saturday night."

He closed his eyes and swallowed. "I'm sorry about the way I acted, Danielle. I said some harsh things, but I didn't mean to hurt you."

"I know, Jack. When I was getting ready for work this morning, I was thinking about how you helped April last night. And I came to a conclusion."

"What's that?"

"I don't want that night to be how I remember you. I've lost too much in my life, and I don't want to lose you as a friend."

He flinched as a knifelike pain pierced his chest and he bit down on his lip. "I don't want that, either."

"So…"

He waited before he spoke. "What?"

"You know next week is Thanksgiving. I'm not going to see my parents, since I'll be moving there in a few weeks. I wondered if you would like to celebrate the holiday with me."

His heart fluttered, and he wished he could see her face. He knew it had taken a lot of courage for her to call knowing she risked the possibility he might reject her offer. He took a deep breath. "I can't."

There was a rustle of movement on the other end of the line. "Oh, I see. Well, if you don't want to I understand. I'm sorry, I…"

He sat up straighter. "No, wait. It's not that I don't want to. I can't, because that's my only day off, and I need to go to Asheville to see my mother."

"Oh, then I understand. Being with your mother is very important. I hope she'll know you're there."

He gritted his teeth and warned himself about

speaking the words that lodged in his throat. It was no use. He had to be with her again before she left. "Would you come with me to Asheville?"

She gasped. "Do you really want me to?"

"Yes, I'd like for you to meet my mother. I have to warn you, though, it won't be a happy visit. She won't understand who I am and why we're there. If you'd rather not go, it's okay."

"No, I want to go. What time will you pick me up?"

"I'll be there about nine o'clock. We'll drive over to Asheville and get there in time to visit before lunch."

She laughed, and the sound flowed over him like a warm breath of air. "I'll see you then, Jack. Goodbye."

"Goodbye, Danielle."

He sat staring at his phone after he'd disconnected the call. His mind told him he should never have invited her, but his heart knew differently. Even if his mother didn't recognize him, he wanted to spend Thanksgiving with someone he cared about. With his mother hidden in the shell of the woman who sat in the nursing home, Danielle was the only other person he could share that with.

Danielle placed the telephone on the handset and buried her face in her hands. What had she done? She'd practically thrown herself at Jack. Never in her life had she been so brazen. When she'd gotten home last night, she realized she couldn't leave Webster Falls without making an attempt to heal the rift between them.

She leaned back in her chair and smiled. He didn't seem upset, so maybe he had been waiting for her to make the first step. Now that she had, all she could was pray that their trip to Asheville would turn out all right.

She scooped up the stack of file folders containing the plans for the fundraiser, stood and walked to her office door. Jeff and Nathan would be waiting, and she needed to get this meeting over. There were still many details to be worked out, and she had little time left.

When she entered Jeff's outer office, Betty peered over the glasses perched on the end of her nose and waved her on through. "They're waiting."

"Thanks," she called over her shoulder and entered Jeff's office.

Jeff rose from behind his desk, and Nathan pushed up from the chair where he sat. They both smiled, but Danielle could see lines of fatigue around their eyes. Nathan pointed to the chair next to him. "Sit here, Danielle."

She smiled and slipped into the wingback chair. Crossing her legs, she positioned the folders on her knee and opened the first one. "I know you have other things on your mind this morning, so I'll be brief.

Who do you want to take over Landon's duties for the fundraiser?"

The words had no sooner left her mouth than Nathan jumped up and began to pace back and forth beside Jeff's desk. "This latest scandal could be the ruin of the school. A stalker! Who would have thought Landon Morse would stoop to endangering our students? I can imagine half our students not returning after Christmas break."

Jeff sighed, and Danielle thought the two had probably discussed the situation at length before she arrived. "Please, Nathan. We've been through all this."

Nathan stopped and stared at Danielle. "Jeff's right. We have to look at this in a positive way. We've suspended Landon with pay. If the charges are proved, he'll be terminated." He spread his hands and shrugged. "That's all we can do."

Danielle nodded. "Of course it is. Nobody here is responsible for Landon's actions. I'm sure the students and their parents will realize that you've done what's required by the school."

Jeff dropped the pen he held to his desk and stood. "Danielle's right, Nathan. There's nothing else we can do at this point." He turned to Danielle. "With a student's murder and now a teacher accused of stalking and assault, we've never had such a year. There's more riding on this fundraiser than ever, and we're looking to you to make it the best ever. We have to assure our donors they have nothing to worry about."

A shiver ran up Danielle's spine at Jeff's ominous tone. He seemed to be telling her that the survival of the school rested with her. "I'll do my best to make that happen."

"We know you will," Nathan said. He glanced at the folders and settled back in his chair. "Now let's hear the final plans for the evening."

Thirty minutes later Danielle entered her office, dropped the folders onto her desk and breathed a sigh of relief that Jeff and Nathan had approved every detail. Although the meeting had gone well, she still had many last-minute details to address.

Just as she reached for her desk calendar, someone knocked at the door. "Come in." Nathan stepped into the room. "Did you need something else?" she asked.

He smiled and nodded. "I wanted to speak with you privately for a moment, if it's all right."

"Of course." She pointed to a chair. "Do you want to sit?"

He shook his head. "No. I need to stand for what I have to say."

Danielle's face warmed, and the hairs on the back of her neck stood up. In all the years she'd known Nathan, she'd never seen him the way he looked now. His dark gaze flitted over her and left a trail of fire across her face. His dark hair, usually combed in place, tumbled over his forehead. His chest rose with the short puffs of breath he exhaled. Only one word described how he looked—tortured.

He reached out and caressed her cheek. "Why are you leaving, Danielle?"

She took a step back against the front of her desk. He moved forward, making her a prisoner between him and the desk. She smiled, but her lips trembled. "I want to work with my parents, Nathan."

He shook his head. "Please don't go. I can't bear for you to leave."

She wiggled past him and walked behind her desk. "I'm sure you'll find someone better to fill my job."

He leaned over and flattened his palms on the desk. "I'll never find anyone to replace you, Danielle. I love you."

Danielle gasped and stared at him in disbelief. "You're not serious."

He nodded, and then his face hardened. "I am. I've loved you since the day you walked into that interview room as an aspiring student. We've been through a lot together, and I've always tried to be there for you."

"You've been wonderful to me, Nathan."

He smiled. "Then marry me and stay at Webster. You may not love me now, but you'll come to after we're married. I'll make you happy. I promise."

Danielle stared at the man who had been like a second father to her ever since she came to Webster as a student. She'd never guessed how he felt, and she didn't want to hurt him after all he'd done to help her. Walking back to him, she took his hands in hers.

"Nathan, you are one of the dearest friends I'll ever have, but I can't marry you. You need a woman who loves you with passion, not someone who thinks of you as a friend. Besides, I don't think I'll ever marry."

He pulled his hands free and stepped back. "Is it that policeman? Are you in love with him?"

She hesitated before she answered. "If I am, it doesn't matter. There's no future for Jack and me. I'm going home to try to forget all the bad memories from here."

His shoulders slumped. "Am I one of those bad memories?"

"Oh, no. You're one of the best ones of all my years at Webster."

He smiled. "Then maybe there's hope for me yet. Would you mind if I visited you in Atlanta after you leave?"

"I'd like that very much, and so would my parents."

He smiled and reached for her hand. Bringing it to his lips, he squeezed her fingers and kissed the back of her hand. He straightened as the office door opened.

Danielle glanced over his shoulder as Flynn Carter stepped into the room. His eyes grew wide. "Oh, excuse me, Dr. Tyler. I didn't know you were busy."

She pulled her hand from Nathan's grasp and

smiled. "It's okay, Flynn. Can I help you with something?"

His gaze darted from Nathan to her. "I just wanted you to know I've decided not to go home for Thanksgiving. I'm going to stay on campus and try to catch up on the classwork I missed the week I was absent. If you have anything you need me to work on, I'll be glad to do it."

Danielle nodded. "There's lots to do with the fundraiser coming up. I'll put together a list and leave it on your desk."

He nodded. "Thanks. Now I'll get out of here. Like I said, I'm sorry to interrupt."

When he'd closed the door, Danielle let out a long breath. "I have trouble every time I'm around Flynn."

Nathan frowned. "What do you mean?"

She shrugged and crossed her arms. "I know it's silly, but I keep thinking if it wasn't for him Tricia might still be alive. I know she made the decision to pose for that Web site, but he shouldn't have put her in that danger. I've spent many sleepless nights trying to overcome my feelings about him, but it's been difficult."

Nathan glanced in the direction of the door and stood in thought for a moment. "Maybe I made a mistake in letting him come back to school."

Danielle's eyes grew wide. "Oh, no. I'm glad you did. I'll work out my feelings about Flynn in time."

Nathan smiled. "I'm sure you will. And maybe you'll also work out your feelings about me. At least I hope so."

Before she could answer, he turned and walked from the room. Danielle stared after him. This morning had certainly been surprising. She'd practically thrown herself at one man and rejected another. Of the two she suspected Nathan might be the better choice. With him there'd never be any worry about money, but she'd never cared about wealth. Nathan's kind nature made him look almost angelic when compared to Jack's remote and at times sullen approach to life.

She had to admit that Nathan had a lot of characteristics that would make him a wonderful husband. Knowing all this made no difference. Jack was the one she wanted.

EIGHTEEN

Danielle pulled the living room curtain back and peered out at dark clouds hovering over the rolling mountain peaks. She'd hoped for clear weather on this Thanksgiving Day for the trip to Asheville. Interstate 40's winding road toward Asheville snaked through valleys guarded by the steep mountainsides of the range. Hanging rocks loosened by bad weather could trigger massive landslides without warning.

She let the curtain drift from her hand. Why was she concerned about the weather? She hadn't heard from Jack in the week since her telephone call. He probably wouldn't even show up today.

A car door slammed out front, and she knew he was here. Grabbing her jacket, she ran to the door and had it open before he could knock. His eyes sparkled, and the tired lines in his face had disappeared.

"Hello, Jack. I was beginning to think you weren't coming."

"Sorry. I slept a little later this morning. Are you ready to go?"

She nodded, and they hurried to the car as raindrops began to fall. He held the door for her and ran around to the driver's side. Just as he climbed inside, a strong wind shook the vehicle and sheets of rain pounded the windshield.

Danielle leaned forward and stared through the windshield. "Do you think we'll be in this weather all the way to Asheville?"

Before he could answer, his cell phone rang, and he pulled it from his pocket. "Excuse me, Danielle. This is Will. I need to take it." He flipped the phone open. "Hello, Will. What's up?"

The sparkle she'd seen in his eyes earlier grew duller by the moment as he listened. He chewed on his bottom lip and cast a quick glance at her from time to time. Danielle's stomach fluttered with the certainty that something was terribly wrong.

"I was just about to leave town, but I'll be right there. See you in a few minutes."

He closed the phone and turned to Danielle. "I'm afraid our trip to Asheville is going to have to wait."

"What's happened, Jack?"

He put his elbow on the steering wheel and rubbed his eyes, then turned to her. "I'm sorry to have to tell you this, Danielle, but…"

Chills ran up her spine, and she grabbed his arm. "Please don't tell me something's happened to someone else I know."

He nodded. "It's Flynn. An officer found him in his car with a suicide note that he'd killed Tricia."

Her body began to shake, and tears rolled down her face. "Not another one," she wailed.

Jack jumped out of the car, rushed around to her side and pulled her from the car. They hurried through the driving rain toward the house. When they stood on the porch, he wrapped his arms around her. She buried her face in his chest and cried out her rage at yet another unnecessary death.

When she'd calmed, he looked down at her. "I have to go to the station. Let me get you inside."

She wiped her hands across her face and blinked. "You go on, Jack. I have to see if Nathan and Jeff have heard this latest news. I'll probably have to go to the school."

He held her at arms' length and studied her face. "Are you sure?"

She nodded. "I'm okay. I should be used to this by now. Everybody around me dies. You'd better watch yourself, Jack. You could be next."

She pushed away from him, whirled and dashed inside the house.

Danielle had wanted this last day with Jack, but it wasn't to be. Tragedy had struck another student at

Webster University and left her wondering why death followed her.

There was something about Webster's campus that spawned evil, and she was glad she was leaving. She needed to stay as far away from that place as possible. However, there a downside to her leaving. She didn't know what she'd do when Jack wasn't nearby anymore.

Silence covered the halls of Webster University's Administration Building the day after Thanksgiving. With students and faculty gone for the holiday, the deserted building reminded Danielle of a mausoleum. She stopped in the doorway of Jeff's office and surveyed the all-too-familiar scene.

Jeff sat behind his desk, one elbow on his desk and his chin propped on his fist. Nathan slumped in a chair beside him, and Jack sat facing them. The only difference today was that Landon wasn't in attendance.

They all rose as she walked into the room. "Good morning, Danielle," Jeff said. "I'm sorry to bring you in on a holiday weekend, but Detective Denton wanted to bring us up to date on Flynn's death."

She could hardly meet their gazes. Just days ago she'd voiced her feelings about Flynn putting Tricia in danger, and now she'd found out he was the killer all along. She still found it hard to believe that the boy who had worked in her office could be a killer. But then she didn't know what might have prompted his actions.

Nathan motioned to the chair next to him. "Sit here, Danielle."

She nodded and eased into the chair, then glanced up at Jack. His eyes narrowed, and his gaze raked her before he turned back to Jeff. "I wanted to let you know that Carter's body is being sent to Asheville for an autopsy this morning. His parents have been notified and will make arrangements for the body to be returned to California when it's released."

Jeff bit down on his lip. "We've been in touch with the family, too. We've assured them we'll assist them any way we can."

Danielle scooted to the edge of her chair. "I understand the reason for Tricia's body being sent for an autopsy. She was a murder victim, and the police needed all the information they could get about her death. But why Flynn? You already know his wound was self-inflicted."

Jack shook his head. "It's standard procedure. In Flynn's case the autopsy will help us rule out the possibility of murder."

Nathan's eyes grew wide. "Murder? But I thought the police had ruled it suicide."

"Not yet. It's a suspected suicide, but we have to be sure. I did have one question I wanted to ask." He glanced from one to the other. "Do any of you know whether Carter was left- or right-handed?"

"I know," Danielle answered. "He was left-handed. He was always complaining that the world is arranged for right-handed people, and he was at a disadvantage in whatever he did. Why do you ask?"

Jack shrugged. "Just part of the investigation." He pushed up from his chair. "By the way, Landon Morse made bail the day before Thanksgiving."

Danielle gasped. "Then he was out of jail when Flynn died."

"That's right." He turned to Jeff. "If it's all right, I'd like to search his office while I'm here."

"Are you looking for anything in particular?"

"No. It's just a hunch."

Jeff stood. "Then go right ahead." He held out a key ring. "Danielle can show you where it is."

Jack's forehead wrinkled. "I think you should come, too. Morse is still under investigation, and I'd like your permission if I find anything I need to take."

Jeff glanced at Nathan. "Then why don't we all go?"

Nathan nodded, and they filed from the room. Danielle strode down the hallway, aware that Jack walked beside her, but she didn't look at him. When they reached Landon's office, Jeff stepped around her and unlocked the door.

Once inside, Jack went to Landon's desk, sat down

and opened the top drawer. Danielle walked to the window and looked out onto the quadrangle. She turned back to Nathan. "I've never noticed before that Landon's office faces the quadrangle."

Nathan stepped up beside her and gave a snort of disgust. "I suppose he had his own view of all the girls going to class. I can't believe we brought somebody like him back to this campus."

Danielle turned at the sound of Jack opening Landon's storage closet. A jacket hung inside and books and music lined the shelves. Jack stood on tiptoe and ran his hand along the top shelf. He frowned and stretched taller.

"What's this?"

Danielle and Nathan turned as Jack pulled a laptop from the back of the shelf. Jeff stepped closer. "That's Landon's laptop. Every teacher has one they can take home."

Jack set the computer on the desk and opened it. He started to press the power button but hesitated. Closing it again, he looked up at Jeff. "I don't think our tech guys checked a laptop in Morse's office when they were here. Do you mind if I take this one with me?"

Jeff nodded. "Of course."

Jack stood and picked up the computer. "I'll let you know if we find anything interesting on it. Now I need to get back to headquarters."

They stepped from the office into the hallway and walked back toward the front of the building. When they reached Jeff's office, he shook Jack's hand. "I'm sorry Webster has caused you so much trouble, Detective Denton. I hope everything will soon be brought to a conclusion."

Nathan nodded. "So do I. Jeff and I have some matters to discuss. Danielle, there's no need for you to stay. Go on and enjoy what's left of your holiday."

She and Jack walked down the hallway toward the front door. When they stepped outside, he stopped and faced her. "I'm sorry we didn't get to go to Asheville yesterday. I wanted you to meet my mother."

Danielle tried to smile, but something in his eyes told her this was his goodbye to her. "I feel like I already know her, Jack."

He frowned. "How?"

"Because she raised a nice son. Only a special woman could have done that." She paused a moment and took in every detail of his face. "I'm going to miss you, Jack."

"I'm going to miss you, too."

He leaned closer, and she took a step toward him. His eyes bored into her. She closed her eyes and turned her face up to him. Her lips burned, awaiting Jack's first kiss. The fire that consumed her dwindled to embers as his lips grazed her cheek.

"Goodbye, Danielle," he whispered.

She rocked back and forth in disbelief as the sound of his footsteps faded away. Finally she opened her eyes and stared in the direction he'd disappeared. Her heart shriveled just like the dried leaves whirling in the wind across the campus. She felt as lifeless and wrinkled as they appeared, and she doubted if she would ever feel alive again.

Anger shot through her, and she blinked back tears. What was the matter with her? She was about to embark on a journey that would improve the lives of destitute people in Africa. She was going to serve in the name of her Lord. Why should she be upset over a man who clearly had no feelings for her? She had a higher calling to answer, and that meant leaving this town and everybody in it far behind.

NINETEEN

Jack hurled the breaking-and-entering report into the desk's top drawer and slammed it closed. He jumped to his feet and covered the distance to the window in two strides. With a yank of the cord, the blinds shot to the top of the sill, and he stared outside.

No matter how hard he tried to concentrate, his thoughts kept returning to Danielle. He hadn't seen her or spoken with her since their parting at Webster a week ago.

Blood pounded in his temples at the memory of her closed eyes and lips raised, waiting for a kiss. He'd wanted to pull her to him and promise he'd never let her go, but in the end he'd retreated. Standard procedure for him. No involvement. It hurt too much. Jack raked his hand through his hair. Nothing could hurt much worse than the knifelike pain that clawed inside his chest.

The door to his office burst open, and Will rushed in. "Hey, man, we just got the report on Flynn Carter's body from the state lab. It looks like the death wasn't suicide. From the angle of the shot they said it was highly suspicious a left-handed person could shoot himself at that particular spot on the right side of the head."

Jack frowned. "Highly suspicious, but not impossible?"

"That's right, but here's the clincher. There was no gunshot residue on Carter's hands and none of his DNA on the gun. Looks like we have a murder here."

Jack rubbed his hands over his eyes. "Another one to add to the list. When is this killer going to stop?"

"Well, I saved the best for last. The tech guys came back with their report on Landon Morse's computer. You remember the encore message that was sent to Carter's Web site the day of Tricia Peterson's murder?"

"Yeah."

"It came from Morse's laptop. That's why the tech guys couldn't find the computer when they checked all of them at the school. Morse had it hidden."

Jack sat down on the edge of his desk and shook his head. "Wow. Maybe we're closer to solving this case than we thought."

Will stuck his hands in his pocket and nodded. "Well, there is one more little piece of evidence I haven't told you yet. Our tech guys also found a deleted e-mail message to Flynn Carter on Morse's computer. It was from an online account, not his school account. The user name was Flasher, and the message asked Carter to meet him at the Laurel Falls parking lot. He said he had some information about Tricia's death."

Jack gave a low whistle. "I guess that's enough evidence to arrest Morse for the deaths of Tricia Peterson and Flynn Carter. I wish we could connect him to Jennifer McCaslin."

Jack grabbed his jacket off the coatrack beside his desk. "Let's go arrest Landon Morse."

They walked to the parking lot and climbed into Will's car. As they pulled from the lot, Jack thought of Danielle. With Morse's arrest she might finally have some peace.

Next week she would be leaving Webster Falls. If they could get Morse to confess to all the unsolved murders, then he could give her some closure to her nightmares.

Danielle punched the last grade into the computer and clicked out of the program. She gripped the arms of her chair and tapped her index fingers on the vinyl covering. How could she have let Jeff talk her into taking over Landon's music appreciation class while he was suspended? She had more than enough to do just to get ready for the fundraiser, which was only four days away.

She glared at the computer a moment. Yawning, she fought the urge to lay her head on her arms and take a quick nap. With a wriggle of her shoulders she straightened in her chair. Even if her responsibilities appeared huge at the moment she could get through this. Exams would be over in a few days, and all her commitments to Webster would be fulfilled—Tuesday night, the fundraiser and Wednesday morning, leave for home.

A soft knock at her office door caught her attention. "Come in."

The door inched open, and Jeff stuck his head around the side. "May I come in?"

She rose from her chair. "Of course."

He stepped into the room and stopped in front of her desk. His big grin and the cocky tilt of his head made him look like a little boy bursting to reveal a secret. "I've got news."

"What is it?"

"I just had a call from Detective Denton. They've arrested Landon Morse for the murders of Tricia and Flynn."

The breath left her body, and she fell down into her chair. Her mouth gaped open as she stared up at him. "Murder? I wasn't surprised at the stalking arrest, but murder." Even to her ears the statement sounded like a question. She couldn't believe Landon capable of the brutality Tricia and Flynn had suffered.

He sat down on the corner of her desk. "I'll tell you what Detective Denton told me."

She listened in disbelief as Jeff related the mounting evidence against Landon. When he'd finished, he spread his hands. "That's all he said, but it seems like they have this case tied up."

"And Jennifer? What about her murder?"

Jeff's eyes narrowed, and he shook his head. "They can't find anything to connect him to that murder. They think Tricia's death was a copycat of what happened here ten years ago. We may never know who killed Jennifer."

Danielle hesitated a moment before she spoke again. "Did Detective Denton say anything else?"

Jeff shook his head. "He said he'd be in touch as the trial date draws near, but that could be months away. Until then, Landon is in jail without bail."

Danielle sighed. "I thought what Landon did to April was reprehensible, but I didn't think of him as a killer."

Jeff pushed off the desk. "Neither did I, but you never can tell what another person is like."

"Have you told Nathan?"

"I called him. He's been under the weather this week and hasn't been coming to the campus. I think he wants to be well for the fundraiser on Tuesday night."

The stack of work caught Danielle's eye, and she pointed to it. "If I don't get to work, there won't be a fundraiser. Thanks for coming by to tell me, Jeff."

"I thought you'd want to know." He glanced over his shoulder as he walked toward the door. "Oh, by the way, Detective Denton asked me about the fundraiser. I got the impression he was fishing for an invitation, so I asked him to come. I suppose it's the least I could do after all he's done to help the university."

Danielle's heart thudded like a bass drum. "What did he say?"

Jeff shrugged. "Not much. You know how he is. He just thanked me for the invitation."

Danielle waited for Jeff to close the door behind him before she doubled her fist and banged the desktop. Why was Jack doing this to her? She knew he liked her. His actions, though, resembled a callous man who didn't care who he hurt. She'd thought she could find the real Jack underneath the self-imposed armor he wore, but she'd failed.

She hoped she never saw him again.

On Tuesday night Jack stood outside the ballroom in the Nathan Webster Pavilion and debated on whether or not to enter. Inside he could hear the string quartet performing above the low hum of conversation. He'd wrestled all day with the decision of what to do and finally had given in and come in hopes of catching one last glimpse of Danielle.

She'd be leaving Webster Falls tomorrow. All he wanted was to see her once more. He'd slip into the room, mingle with the guests until he spotted her and then leave. If all went as planned, she'd never know he'd been there. Taking a deep breath, he pushed the door open and eased into the room.

Flickering candles adorned the white-draped tables that covered the room. Small groups of ladies in long dresses and men in tuxedoes stood talking while the string quartet serenaded them with pre-dinner music. Their elegant attire and relaxed mannerisms screamed money.

Jack glanced down at the suit he wore and realized how underdressed he was. He gritted his teeth and shook his head. When would he ever learn? He didn't belong with people like Danielle's friends.

He whirled to leave, but she blocked his path. "Hello, Jack. Leaving already?"

The vision of her standing there in the soft light took his breath away. The strapless white evening gown she wore sheathed her body as if it had been molded for a perfect fit. A long shimmering stole of the same material draped her shoulders. He'd never seen anyone as beautiful in his life.

"H-how did you know I was here?"

She smiled. "I saw you come in and thought I'd speak to you."

He tried to ease around her, but she moved in front of him. He gulped and nodded. "I just dropped by for a moment to see how the fundraiser was going." He shoved his hands into his pockets and glanced around the room. "Your friends are very nice-looking people."

Danielle chuckled. "They're not my friends, Jack. I know most of the people in this room from seeing their names on our donations list."

He took a deep breath. "Then maybe you'll raise a lot of money tonight."

"That's the plan."

The sad smile she directed at him pricked his heart. "Danielle, I wish I could have gotten Morse to confess to Jennifer's murder before you left, but he refuses. He insists he hasn't killed anybody."

She nodded. "Thank you for trying. You know I'm leaving tomorrow."

"I know."

"My suitcases are packed, and the movers will be there early in the morning to load the furniture."

"I hope you'll be happy working with your parents."

Tears welled in her eyes. "And I hope you'll be happy, Jack. One of these days you're going to find out that you don't have to shoulder all your problems alone. You can have peace about the past."

He shook his head. "If you're talking about God again, I don't think so. I don't know anything He's ever done for me."

She stared into his eyes for a moment before she

frowned. "There are many things about you that sadden me, Jack, but that last statement is the saddest of all. At some point in your life, you're going to be faced with something you can't handle. I hope you change your mind then."

Before he could stop her, she whirled and hurried across the room. He watched her go and tried to memorize every detail about her appearance. It would be all he had in the coming days to ease the loss that already gouged at his heart.

Danielle pushed through the swinging door into the kitchen. Food service personnel bustled about the room putting the last-minute touches on the salads that waited on trays to be transported to the guests' tables. No one appeared to notice her.

She cracked the door open just enough to give her a view of where she and Jack had stood and caught a glimpse of him leaving the room. The smell of cooking food that had seemed so enticing when it drifted through the dining room suddenly overpowered her, and she struggled to breathe. The walls began to slant, and the floor spun underneath her feet.

Fearing that she was about to faint, she stumbled across the room and escaped into the fresh air of the night. Outside on the driveway back of the building, she inhaled large gulps of air until her head cleared.

The door behind her opened, and she glanced

around to see Nathan approaching. His forehead wrinkled, and concern shone in his eyes. "Danielle, are you all right? I saw you leave the dining room, and I was afraid you were sick."

She smiled, but her lips trembled. "I'm fine, Nathan. It got too stuffy in there, and I felt a little faint. I'm okay now."

He sighed. "I'm glad. You frightened me. Especially since you were talking to Detective Denton. I was afraid he'd said something to upset you."

She turned her head away so her face didn't reveal her anguish. "He came by to see how the fundraiser was going. He said he had hoped to get Landon to confess to Jennifer's murder, but he hasn't."

Nathan stepped up beside her. "Don't think about Jennifer or Tricia or Flynn tonight. You should be enjoying your accomplishment of making this event a success." He held out a cup of punch. "I brought this to you. I thought we might toast your achievement together."

She took the glass and stared at it before she looked up at him. "I really didn't do anything. It was everybody helping me that made it all come together."

He raised his cup. "Then let's toast all who worked on the event."

She smiled and tapped his cup. "I can do that."

Danielle took a sip and then another. "This is really good."

He nodded. "Yes. It's a special batch I made just for you. Drink it all up."

Raising the cup, she drained it. The fire inside her ebbed, and she smiled. "I think it's relaxed me a lot."

A door clanged shut behind them. One of the kitchen staff walked to the container at the back of the building and tossed some trash inside. A long, white apron hung to his ankles, and he straightened it before he turned and disappeared into the building.

The ground dipped from under her, and Danielle grabbed for Nathan's arm. With a chuckle he took the cup from her and set it down on the ground. "Aren't you feeling well, my dear?"

Danielle pressed her hand to her forehead. "I'm just a little dizzy."

Taking her hand in his, he stared into her eyes. "Don't worry. I'll take care of you."

She swayed toward him. "I'm all right. You don't need to take care of me."

"Oh, but I do. You're a wonderful woman, Danielle, and a very talented one. I can't tell you how much it's meant to me to see you working so hard for the school my family founded."

She reeled to the right, but his hand held her tightly. "Thank you."

"I can see it continuing after we're married. You'll be by my side every day helping make this institution one of the best in the country."

Her eyelids drooped, and she blinked. "Married?" The words sounded as if they came from far away.

Nathan took her arm and nudged her toward the parking lot. "That's right, my darling. You've never known how much I love you, but I'm about to give you the world. Anything you want is possible. I'm going to make your life so grand you'll wonder why you didn't fall in love with me earlier."

She stumbled, but he caught her and wrapped his arm around her waist. "Love you? But I love Jack." She stopped and shook her head. "No, not Jack."

What was happening to her? All she wanted was to lie down and sleep, close her eyes and not worry about Jack or Nathan. Her eyes grew wide. Nathan said they were going to be married.

His arm tightened, and she stared into his rage-filled face. "Don't ever mention that detective's name to me again. He's gone from our lives. You are mine, and I am claiming you tonight."

She tried to push against his chest, but her fingers kept slipping. Her knees grew weaker, and she thought she might collapse at any moment. She sagged against Nathan, and he half carried, half dragged her across the parking lot.

She tried to keep her eyes open, but they wouldn't cooperate. A soft click like a lock releasing sounded from somewhere nearby, and she wondered what it was. She must have drifted off because when she opened her eyes, she lay on a flat surface on her side. She tried to straighten her bent knees, but her feet hit against some sort of wall.

Nathan leaned over her. "I have to go see to my guests. Since you're ill, I'll make your apologies. When the dinner's over, we'll go home. You're going to love it there."

She reached up and clutched at his shirt. "N-N-Nathan," she moaned.

He kissed her hand and tucked her arm against her side. "I've always loved you, Danielle." He reached over her, picked up something and laid it next to her. "Here's another rose for you, darling. You bring joy to my life."

"Y-y-you s-sent the r-roses?"

"Everything I've done has been for you. Now it's your turn to make me happy."

She tried to get up, but he pushed her back down. He reached above her and pulled something toward her. She squinted through bleary eyes to see what he was doing.

"Sleep well, my darling. I'll wake you later."

Darkness, accompanied by a loud thump, descended around her as if a veil had dropped. She tried to push up, but her head struck something hard. She sank back and tried to roll over, but her body wouldn't move.

The rough surface underneath where she lay

scratched at her body, and she ran her fingers along its surface. Carpet. Then she touched a piece of metal and inched her fingers upward.

Exhausted, she lay still, unable to move any more. Her eyes closed and popped open before they closed again in resignation. There was no escape.

Before unconsciousness overtook her, she said a quick prayer that somehow Jack would find her. How he would, she didn't know. Only God and Nathan knew she was imprisoned in the trunk of a car.

TWENTY

Jack hadn't slept all night. The memory of Danielle hurrying toward the kitchen had kept him awake. He'd almost called her cell phone this morning to tell her goodbye, but he'd changed his mind after he'd dialed the first number. He had taken one liberty on his way to work and driven by her house. A moving van sat out front, but he didn't see her car. It might have been behind the house.

He tapped the pencil he held on his desk and stared into space. She should be gone by now. He slapped his palms on his desk. So much for his relationship with Danielle Tyler. Now he needed to get to work, take his mind off her. He reached over and booted his computer just as the phone rang.

"Hello."

"Jack," Mary the dispatcher said, "I have a Kenny Tyler from Atlanta on the line, and he insists on talking to you and no one else."

Jack jerked upright in his chair and grasped the receiver tighter. "Put him on."

"Hello, Mr. Tyler. This is Jack Denton."

"Jack, have you seen Danielle this morning?"

"No, I saw her last night. Why?"

"We can't reach her, and I'm worried."

Jack's heart pounded. "Has something happened?"

"Yes. We got a text message from her this morning. She said she'd decided not to come home after all. Said she needed some time to think. We tried to call her, but her phone keeps going to voice mail. We've left a dozen messages, but she hasn't returned any."

"If she wants to be alone, she might ignore your calls."

"No, not Danielle. She'd know how worried we'd be. She would never text us such a message. We also got a call from the moving company I hired."

Jack sat up straighter. "What did they say?"

"They went to her house at the time she'd told them to come, but she wasn't there. They waited for several hours, but she never showed up." The man dissolved into tears. "We're scared, Jack. What if she's in the house hurt, or God forbid dead?"

"Now let's not panic, Mr. Tyler. I'll go to her house and check on her."

"There's a key under the big flowerpot in the corner of the porch. Let yourself in."

"I will. Give me your phone number, and I'll call you when I know anything. Don't worry. I'll find her."

Jack hoped his words sounded more confident than he felt.

Kenny told him the number, and he programmed it into his cell phone.

"Please, Jack. Call us as soon as you know anything. We're going crazy here."

Jack swallowed. "I will. I'll talk to you in a little while."

Jack hung up, grabbed his jacket and ran down the hall. "I'm on my way to Dr. Danielle Tyler's house. Her parents can't reach her and are worried," he yelled to Mary as he dashed by.

Jumping into his car, he resisted the urge to turn on the siren. This call wouldn't be classified an emergency by anyone else. To him, though, it ranked up there with his worst fears. From the moment Kenny Tyler began to speak, Jack's blood had turned cold. Call it a hunch, a premonition, whatever. He knew something had happened to Danielle.

When he arrived at her house, he bounded up the steps in two leaps and had the front door open in seconds. A quick search through the rooms confirmed what he had expected—she was nowhere to be found. In the bathroom, two towels and a washcloth hung on the shower door as if they'd been placed there to dry after bathing. Her makeup lay scattered across the vanity, but the bedroom revealed something else he suspected. Her bed hadn't been slept in. She hadn't made it home from the fund-raiser the night before.

Whirling around, he ran from the house, jumped in his car and raced toward the university. When he drove into the parking lot back of the Nathan Webster Pavilion, his heart sank to his stomach. Danielle's car sat in the same spot where he had seen it last night. A quick search of the unlocked car yielded nothing.

Pulling his cell phone from his pocket, he punched Jeff Newman's number and waited for an answer.

"Dr. Newman's office. May I help you?"

"Betty, this is Jack Denton. May I speak with Dr. Newman?"

"I'm sorry, Detective Denton. He hasn't come in yet. Do you want to leave a message?"

Jack raked his hand through his hair. "How about Mr. Webster? Is he in yet?"

"No, I'm sorry. Mr. Webster is taking the day off. I think he needed to recuperate from the big fundraiser last night. Dr. Newman will probably be here within the hour if you want to call back."

"Thanks. I'll do that."

Jack flipped the phone closed and jogged across the parking lot toward the back of the building. When he'd last seen Danielle, she was walking into the kitchen. Maybe some of the staff working this morning had noticed her last night.

He pulled the kitchen door open and stepped inside. One woman in a white uniform turned from grating cheese and another looked up from a pot bubbling on the stove. A third peeked around the corner from what appeared to be the dish room.

Jack flashed his badge. "My name is Detective Jack Denton. I need to ask you ladies some questions."

They exchanged quick glances before they formed a semicircle around him. The oldest of the three nodded. "What can we do for you?"

"Do you ladies know Dr. Danielle Tyler, the Dean of Students here?"

Their heads bobbed in unison. "Sweetest lady on staff. We like to see her come to the dining room."

"Were any of you working last night's fundraiser?"

Again the three heads nodded.

"Did you see her in the kitchen last night?"

At this question, all three shook their heads. The oldest shrugged. "It was so busy in here, and we had lots of student workers. Sometimes it was so crowded I didn't know who was here, but I never saw her in the kitchen."

The back door banged, and a young man walked into the room. He stopped when he saw them. "I'm sorry. Am I interrupting something?"

One of the ladies motioned for him to join them. "This is Brandon Putman. He helped us in the kitchen last night."

Jack pulled his badge out again. "I was just asking these ladies if they saw Dr. Danielle Tyler in the kitchen last night."

Brandon smiled. "I saw her. She came from the dining room, walked right by me and went out the back door."

Jack's pulse throbbed. "Was anyone with her?"

Brandon shook his head. "No. She went out alone."

"Did you see her come back in?"

Brandon thought a moment. "No, but Mr. Webster came back."

Jack's eyes grew wide. "What do you mean?"

"About ten minutes after I saw Dr. Tyler pass through here, I had to take some trash outside. I saw her talking to Mr. Webster at the edge of the parking lot. It looked like they might be drinking something."

Jack took a step closer. "Did they look upset or concerned?"

Brandon shook his head. "No. They were just standing there talking. I came on back inside, and after about thirty minutes I saw Mr. Webster walk back through, but I didn't see Dr. Tyler again."

"Thank you for your help." Jack was almost through the door before the last words were out of his mouth.

He raced to his car, jumped in and roared from the parking lot. Now that he knew Danielle had disappeared, he had to find her. The sight of Tricia

Peterson's body flashed before him, and he tried to force it from his mind.

Nothing about Danielle's disappearance made sense yet, but it would. He had to get back to the station and bounce his suspicions off Will. Then they'd decide what to do.

Danielle's eyes blinked open, and she stared upward at the strange panels that covered the ceiling. From somewhere nearby came the soft sound of her parents' music. They sang her favorite song, the one they'd always said was written for her. She smiled. Had she come home? She turned her head and stared at the stark wall beside the bed. It wasn't covered in the flowered paper of the bedroom in her parents' home. Where was she?

Her gaze came to rest on a corner stairway that curved toward the ceiling. She tried to find the upper level of the room, but there didn't seem to be one. The stairs ended at the top of the room.

Her head hurt, and she reached up to massage her temples. She struggled to lift arms that felt as if they weighed one hundred pounds each. The smell of coffee tickled her nose.

"Are you hungry?"

The soft voice shocked her. She wasn't alone. With every bit of strength she could muster she pushed up on her elbows and glanced around. She lay on a bed in a small room. Nathan sat at a table near her feet. A silver tray in front of him held a silver coffeepot and plate of Danish rolls.

Nathan picked up the pot and poured the steaming liquid into a cup. "I thought you would never wake up. I've been checking on you for hours." He inclined his head toward a stereo across the room. "I thought you might like to wake up to your parents' singing. I know how you listen to them all the time."

Danielle glanced down at the blanket covering her and threw it back. She still had on the white dress she'd worn to the fundraiser, but she didn't remember much about the event. She struggled for a memory, and then it all rushed into her head.

She gasped and pushed to her feet. The room revolved around her, and she sat down on the edge of the bed. "Nathan, you drugged and kidnapped me." The accusation escaped her mouth in a rush of words.

He nodded. "It was the only way I could think of to keep you here until I convinced you to marry me." He stood, walked to the bed and handed her a cup of coffee. "Drink this. You'll feel better."

Danielle set the cup on the floor and stood up. Her legs trembled, and she braced them against the side of the bed. "I want to understand why you've done this, Nathan. It doesn't make sense."

He tilted his head to one side and pursed his lips. "You remind me of a child, Danielle. Instead of accepting the wonderful thing that has happened to you, you have to ask why. Sometimes it's better not to know."

"Please, Nathan. You've been my friend for years. Surely you can tell me why you sent the roses and why you've brought me to…" She let her gaze drift across the small enclosure. "Where am I, Nathan?"

"In a fallout shelter. My father had it built years ago. He was convinced the country was going to be bombed, and he wanted us to be safe." He paused. His lips formed a sneer. "That's what he said, but I knew the truth. This place was built for me, because I wasn't perfect enough to be a Webster."

"What do you mean?"

"I lived here a lot. If I got a grass stain on my clothes from playing, if I spilled a glass of milk at dinner, whatever I did to displease them, I was locked in here for punishment. Sometimes it would last for days."

Tears sprang to Danielle's eyes. "I'm so sorry, Nathan."

He smiled and reached for her hand. "It doesn't matter now. It became his turn to live here when he became old and couldn't defend himself. I paid him back with interest."

Danielle shrank from his touch. "Don't talk like that."

He clamped his fingers on her hand and pulled her

back toward him. "From the moment I saw you, I knew you were the one person who would never treat me the way everybody else did. I wanted to make your life the best it could be. I didn't want anything or anybody to cause you any unhappiness."

His wild-eyed stare sent shivers racing through her. Where had the Nathan she'd known for years gone? She had to find that man again. "You've been kind to me. That's why I still don't understand why you've brought me here."

He sighed and released his hold on her hand. He walked across the narrow room, then turned and faced her. "It's time for you to repay me for everything I've done for you. You have to marry me."

Danielle frowned. "Done for me? You mean by giving me a job at Webster?"

He laughed. "Oh, Danielle, you are so naive. Don't you realize what all I've done for you?"

She shook her head. "I don't know what you're talking about."

He twisted his mouth to one side and tapped his forehead with his index finger. "For starters, there's the Webster Scholarship for Graduate study I gave you."

"But Nathan, I only got that scholarship by default after Jennifer was killed."

His eyes glowed. "Exactly."

The truth hit her, and she reeled toward the bed as

if a giant hand had slapped her backward. "You?" she whispered. "You murdered Jennifer?"

He laughed. "It was beautiful, Danielle. You should have heard her beg and plead for her life, but I told her it was no use. She wasn't standing in your way."

A scream tore from Danielle's throat, and she rushed toward him, her hands clawing at him. "You monster!"

Nathan grabbed her hands and circled both her wrists with one hand. She struggled, but his viselike grip held her prisoner. "You're stronger than Jennifer, and Tricia, too, for that matter."

Her knees sagged, but he held her up. "You killed Tricia, too?"

He nodded. "Yes. I saw how upset you were because she reminded you of Jennifer's death. I told her she shouldn't have hurt you that way. She was sorry at the end."

Danielle moved her head from side to side. "How could you? Tricia was such a wonderful girl." She froze in place and stared up at him. "What about Flynn? Did Landon kill him?"

Nathan chuckled. "Landon's guilty of being a pervert and maybe wanting to be a rapist, but he hasn't killed anybody as far as I know."

"But the messages on his computer?"

Nathan's eyes sparkled with excitement. "I thought the police would never find that computer."

"So you killed Flynn, too. Why him?"

A quizzical expression covered his face. "Because you asked me to do it."

Tears rolled from Danielle's eyes. "I didn't."

"But you did. You told me you'd spent many sleepless nights trying to overcome the bad feelings you had for Flynn because he had Tricia pose for that Web site. I knew you wanted him gone so you wouldn't think about it any longer."

Danielle sank to the floor, and Nathan knelt beside her. She looked up at him through tear-filled eyes. "I never wanted you to kill anyone."

"Maybe not Stan, but I knew you wanted the others dead."

If he had kicked her in the stomach, it wouldn't have hurt worse than the pain that knocked the breath from her. She remembered Nathan's visits to her in Chapel Hill when she was in graduate school. Nathan had never approved of Stan, and at the time she'd wondered why.

"Please tell me you didn't murder Stan."

His eyebrows arched. "But I did. I couldn't let him marry you. I was saving you for me."

The horror of what she'd just learned washed over her, and she curled into a fetal position on the floor and began to sob. "I trusted you, Nathan. I thought you were my friend, and you're an evil man. I'm going to see that you pay for what you've done."

He stroked her head. "Now, now, darling. Don't be upset. Everything will look better to you when you've had time to think about what life can be like for you when we're married. I'm rich, Danielle. You can have anything you want, and I promise I'll be a good husband."

She stared up at him. "You're insane. All I want is to get away from you."

He grabbed her arms and jerked her to him. Rage filled his face, and he gritted his teeth. "Don't ever say that to me again, or I'll make you as sorry as Jennifer and Tricia were." He shook her, and her neck popped. "Do you understand me?"

Fear rushed through Danielle, and she nodded. "Yes, Nathan. I understand."

He took a deep breath and released her. "Good. Now I'm going to leave you here to think about what I've said. When you come to your senses, we'll drive over to Asheville and get married by a justice of the peace. My private jet is waiting at the airport to transport us to my villa in Italy for a honeymoon. I'm going to give you the world, Danielle."

She rubbed her arms where his fingers had gouged at her flesh. "I can't go abroad. I don't have my passport."

He chuckled. "I took the liberty of searching your house while you were out one day last week. I found your passport."

Danielle crossed her arms over her stomach and rocked forward. "I can't believe you broke into my house."

"I didn't break in. I used the key under the flower-pot. I go in all the time when you're not there. I enjoy the pleasure I get from being where you live."

She shook her head in dismay. "You're sick, Nathan."

His hand cracked across her face, and she slammed backward, her head striking the concrete floor. "Don't ever say that to me," he screamed. "I want to be good to you, but if I have to punish you I will. And I promise you won't like it. So you decide which you want—a loving husband or a harsh disciplinarian."

He whirled, stormed up the steps to the ceiling, and pushed open a trapdoor at the top. A beam of sunlight shone through the opening for a few seconds before the door slammed back into place.

Reality hit her. Nathan had said she was in a fallout shelter, but it hadn't registered until she saw the small shaft of light. "I'm underground."

She struggled to her feet and stumbled up the steps. When she reached the top, she pushed with all her strength, but the door wouldn't budge. Locked from the outside.

Danielle eased down into the room and fell onto the bed. She still shook from the revelations about the tragedies in her life. Ever since Jennifer's and Stan's deaths, she had distanced herself from relationships because she didn't want to lose someone again. Never would she have suspected Nathan to be the instigator of the evil that touched her life.

She thought of Jack, and fresh tears rolled down her face. She would never see him again, because she would soon be dead. If she refused to marry Nathan, he would most certainly kill her. The slap he'd given her might have been a warning, but she had no doubt a life with him would be filled with much worse than that. So either way, she was going to end up dead.

TWENTY-ONE

Jack burst through the door of Will's office. "We've got a problem."

Will jumped up from behind his computer. "Man, you look awful. What's happened?"

"It's Danielle." Jack dropped down into a chair, propped his elbows on his knees and buried his face in his hands.

Will came around his desk and stood beside him. "What's happened to her?"

"I don't know."

He told Will everything he knew from the time he'd seen her the night before until the present. When he'd finished, Will nodded. "Sounds like an abduction."

Jack pushed out of the chair, his fists clenched. "What if it's the same killer? What if Danielle's next?"

Will clamped his hand on Jack's shoulder. "Now calm down. You're too involved with Danielle to be thinking rationally. We have to approach this like we would any other case."

Jack couldn't deny it anymore. "This is different. I love her."

He expected a wisecrack from Will. Instead he received a sympathetic look and a nod. "I know. That's why we have to be careful and not run around in circles." He stepped back behind his desk. "Something came in this morning that may help."

"What?"

Will picked up a paper with some scribbled notes on it. "I had a call from a detective in Chapel Hill. His captain decided they needed to examine some cold-case files. This guy got the assignment on the Stan Winters case."

"Danielle's fiancé?"

"Yeah. He pulled the file, and he's been going through it. There was a fingerprint from the crime scene in it that had never been identified. He ran it through the state data bank and was surprised when he got a match from one of our murders."

Jack leaned over the desk to read what Will had written. "Which one?"

"There was an unidentified fingerprint on the cell phone underneath Tricia Peterson's body. It matched one in Stan Winters's apartment."

Jack gave a low whistle. "So our killer was also with Stan. Do we have a name to add to the print?"

Will shook his head. "No, and the prints don't match Landon Morse."

"So, the killer knew both victims. It stands to reason that Flynn and Stan were killed by the same person, and it wasn't Landon Morse."

Will sat down behind his desk. "Who else in Webster Falls would have a reason to be in Stan Winters's apartment?"

Jack thought for a moment. "I remember Danielle telling me that Jeff Newman and Nathan Webster both visited her there."

"You think it could be one of them?"

The hair on Jack's neck stood up, and his skin prickled. "Nathan Webster was the last person known to have seen Danielle before she disappeared."

Will jumped up and reached for his jacket. "Then let's go to the school and question him."

Jack held out a hand to stop him. "He's not at school today. Recuperating from the fundraiser the secretary said." His hand trembled, and his chin quivered. "What if he's home because he's done something to Danielle?"

Will's eyes widened. "Let's not think that way yet. Not until we talk to him."

Jack turned and rushed from the office with Will behind. There was no time to waste. Lucky for him he'd attended the party with Danielle at Nathan's home. He knew the way. He only hoped he wasn't too late to save her.

* * *

Thirty minutes later Jack stopped the car at Nathan Webster's mountain home. He was bounding up the front steps before Will could even crawl from the passenger side. Jack pushed the doorbell and waited.

When no one answered, he rang again. This time the door opened. Nathan Webster, wearing khaki pants and a pullover, smiled at them. "Good morning. To what do I owe the honor of a visit from the police?"

Jack restrained himself from throttling the man and demanding to know what had happened to Danielle. "May we speak with you for a moment?"

Nathan motioned them inside. "Of course."

Jack let his gaze wander over the surroundings as he and Will stepped into Nathan's home. Nothing appeared to have been changed since the night of the party. An eerie silence hovered over the room.

In the entry a spiral staircase rose to the upper level of the home. A suitcase sat on the floor next to the bottom step. Jack cocked an eyebrow and inclined his head toward the luggage. "Taking a trip, Mr. Webster?"

Nathan nodded. "I always spend the month of December at my villa in Italy. With the fundraiser over, I don't have any commitments at the school until after the first of the year."

Jack and Will followed Nathan into the den and sat down on the sofa. A fire crackling in the fireplace reminded Jack of the night he and Danielle attended the party. He tried to push the thoughts from his mind and concentrate on his present mission.

Will settled back in the cushions. "When are you planning to leave?"

"Later today." Nathan sat down in a chair facing them, crossed his legs and rested his hands on his knee. "Now, gentlemen, what did you want to talk with me about?"

Jack cleared his throat. "It's about Danielle."

A frown pulled at Nathan's forehead. "I hated to lose her at the university, but I understand her wanting to work with her parents. We're all going to miss her."

Jack cast a quick glance at Will. "Have you seen her this morning?"

Nathan's eyes grew wide. "Why, no. I suppose she's already left for Atlanta."

Jack shook his head. "She didn't come home last night, and her parents can't reach her. They've asked us to find out where she might be."

Nathan sat forward, concern lining his face. "Do you think something has happened to her?"

"We don't know. That's why we're here. You were seen talking with her in the parking lot at the fund-raiser last night. As far as we can determine, that's the last time anybody saw her."

Nathan nodded. "I saw her leave the dining room, and I went to check on her. In fact, I carried her a cup of punch. We talked for a few minutes, and she said she wasn't feeling well and needed to go home. I went back inside and didn't see her again."

Will scooted to the edge of the couch. "What was she doing the last time you saw her?"

"I looked over my shoulder, and she was walking toward her car."

Jack stood and stared down at him. "Are you sure?"

Nathan rose and turned a cold glare at him. "Yes, Detective. If for some reason you think Danielle might be here, I invite you to search this house."

Jack stood and shook his head. "That won't be necessary, Mr. Webster. I'll take your word that she isn't here."

Nathan led them toward the hallway. He held the door open as they stepped onto the porch. "I wouldn't worry about Danielle if I were you. I'm sure she'll turn up soon."

Jack nodded. "I hope so. Thank you for your time and have a good trip to Italy."

"I will." Nathan walked to the edge of the porch as Jack and Will headed toward their car. "Have a Merry Christmas."

Jack slammed the car door and turned the ignition. Beside him Will buckled his seat belt. "What do you think?"

Jack gripped the steering wheel and pulled onto the road. "I don't think I've ever had to work so hard to keep from shoving a guy to the wall and beating him until he told me what I wanted to know." He swallowed and glanced at Will. "He's done something to her."

"What makes you think so?"

"I've seen how he is around Danielle. It's almost like he worships her. If he didn't know where she was, he would have been on the phone calling out every agency in the state to look for her." Jack shook his head. "He knows where she is all right."

Will swiveled in his seat. "Then why didn't we search his house, and why are we going home?"

"We didn't search his house because he wouldn't have offered if she'd been there." Jack made a left turn onto a dirt road that curved into the mountains. "And we're not going home. While I'm finding a hiding place for this car, you alert the department where we are. We're going to sneak back to Webster's house and stake it out. He has to come out sometime, and when he does, maybe he'll lead us to Danielle."

Exhausted, Danielle stumbled down the stairs and fell on the bed. The skin beneath her chipped fingernails burned, and her hands ached from her repeated attempts to get the trapdoor open. She'd explored every inch of her prison, and escape was impossible.

Her head throbbed, probably a side effect from

whatever drug Nathan had given her. She pounded her fists against the mattress. How could she have been so stupid? Even though she'd suspected for several years that Nathan was in love with her, she'd ignored it and continued their friendship. When he told her he loved her weeks ago, she should have sensed the evil in him then, but she was too caught up in her feelings for Jack.

A tear ran from the corner of her eye. "Oh, Jack, please find me."

She covered her eyes with her hands and shook her head. There was no way he could. She didn't even know the location of the fallout shelter. Nathan could have transported her miles away from Webster Falls while she was asleep in the trunk of his car.

And her parents. What about them? They must be frantic because she hadn't called them. They were probably praying for her right now.

She sat up straight and wiped the tears from her face. Her father's words drifted into her mind, and she smiled. He'd often told her of a scripture that helped him get through the tough times in rehab—*Whoever listens to Me will live in safety and be at ease, without fear of harm.*

Her father had listened, and he'd survived. If she was to escape from Nathan, there was only one hope, and that was God.

She slipped to her knees and bowed her head. "Dear God, Even if I don't know where I am, You do. I feel Your presence, and I put my trust in You. Be with me and help me not to fear what may come whatever it may be. I love You, Lord. Amen."

Peace flowed through Danielle's heart, and she rose from her knees. She stretched out on the bed, her arms at her sides, and waited for Nathan to come for her.

Jack and Will had lain on their stomachs and watched from the thick forest beside Nathan's house for two hours, but there had been no movement. What if Webster didn't know Danielle's whereabouts? They might be wasting time here.

Will squirmed. "I'm getting a cramp in my leg, and I'm cold."

"Me, too. What I wouldn't give for a cup of coffee right now."

"And a hamburger."

"And a piece of apple pie."

They looked at each other and grinned. The game they played on stakeouts helped to pass the time, but it did have its drawbacks. It usually increased the hunger pangs in their stomachs.

Will propped himself up on his elbows. "How long are we going to stay here?"

"Any time you want to leave, feel free. I can't until

I know for sure that Webster isn't involved in Danielle's disappearance."

Will cocked an eyebrow. "And how are you going to know that?"

Jack shook his head in resignation and directed his gaze to the house's backyard. A tall birdbath stood in the center of the lawn, and a concrete ring about three feet wide lay to the left of it.

Jack pointed toward the strange yard decoration. "What is that? A birdbath and a sundial?"

Will nodded. "That's what it looks like to me."

A garage sat to the rear of the house, and Jack could see a car inside. If Webster was going anywhere in his vehicle, he'd have to walk right in front of where he and Will hid.

Jack glanced at his watch. Three o'clock. Danielle had now been missing for eighteen hours.

He had to do something. But what? The answer he needed came in the last words she spoke to him. He squinted and tried to remember exactly what she'd said to him at the fundraiser. *At some point in your life, you're going to be faced with something you can't handle. I hope you change your mind then.*

Danielle's words sounded like a prophecy. He was faced with something he couldn't handle alone, and he needed help. She said her faith had gotten her through her rough times, and she'd survived.

He hadn't had the assurance he saw in her, and his

feelings had been like stone until she came into his life. Suddenly he wanted what she had. He wanted to know that he wasn't alone, that someone stood beside him, guiding him and giving him strength to face life's problems.

Jack had thought her faith to be childish, but he was the one who needed to become like a child and trust something he didn't yet understand. After all, that's what faith meant.

God knew where Danielle was, and only God could lead him to her. He closed his eyes and laid his head on his outstretched arms. With a breaking heart he begged God to forgive him and give him the peace He offered. He asked forgiveness for blaming his father for his own shortcomings. And he prayed for forgiveness for rejecting the wonderful gift God had sent him in Danielle. "Please don't punish Danielle for my sins, Lord. I love her so. Please give me the chance to tell her," he whispered.

Will nudged him. "Are you all right?"

He wiped at his eyes and raised his head. "Yeah, I'm fine. Webster said he was leaving for Italy today, so it shouldn't be too long before he makes his move."

Jack directed his focus to the back of the Webster house. Peace flowed through him, and he clenched his teeth. He was ready to face whatever happened next.

TWENTY-TWO

Thirty minutes later Jack snapped his attention to the back door of the Webster home. Nathan emerged carrying the black suitcase Jack had seen in the hallway. Neither Jack nor Will moved a muscle as Nathan walked to the garage, popped the car's trunk and heaved the suitcase inside. Jack hardly dared breathe.

Nathan walked from the garage and stopped at the sundial. He pulled something from his pocket and stared down as if he were in deep thought. After a moment he bent forward and pushed whatever he held into the top of the sundial.

Jack raised his head and peeked through the mountain laurel bush in front of him to get a better view. His eyes grew wide as Nathan grabbed hold of the dome's top and pulled.

The concrete slab slid to the side to reveal a hole in the ground. Jack and Will stared at each other in disbelief as Nathan stepped into the opening and disappeared from view.

"That's no sundial," Jack croaked. "That's some kind of underground bunker."

Will nodded. "Yeah. And that birdbath must be an air vent. Webster has a perfect place for hiding a hostage."

They pushed to their feet and pulled the guns from their belts. "Ready?" Jack whispered.

His heart raced, and his stomach felt as if it was resting in his throat. Will nodded, and Jack breathed one last prayer for Danielle before he and Will crept across the yard.

Danielle sat on the bed, her right hand clutching the wedge-heeled pump she'd worn to the fundraiser. At the first sound of the trapdoor opening, she circled the toe of the shoe with her fingers and slipped her hand behind her back.

Nathan descended the steps and stopped in front of her. He reached out and trailed his fingers down the side of her face. "It's time, my darling. They're waiting at the judge's chambers in Asheville for us. Everything's ready for the wedding."

She stroked the skirt of her dress with her left hand. "This dress is wrinkled. It doesn't look good enough for a wedding."

He chuckled. "Don't worry. My housekeeper is waiting there with a dress. I checked your closet for the right size. I promise you're going to look beautiful." He held out his hand. "Are you ready to go?"

She nodded. "Almost. There's just one more thing."

His eyes sparkled. "What's that?"

"This!"

Danielle sprang from the bed and threw the full force of her weight into the arc of her arm. The wedge heel connected with his temple, and blood spurted down his face. Nathan stumbled back and sank to his knees.

Hiking her long dress to her thighs, she bounded toward the stairs. The concrete floor scrapped at her bare feet, but she raced for the sunlight. The metal of the steps felt cool to her feet, and she moved upward.

About halfway up, a rage-filled roar split the air, and a hand clamped around her ankle. She fell to her knees and clawed at the steps for a hold, but Nathan pulled her back to the floor. Grabbing her by the shoulders, he picked her up and threw her across the room.

She struck the wall behind the bed and bounced onto the mattress. Before she could scramble to her feet, he lunged onto the bed and circled his fingers around her neck. His eyes glared like dark orbs, and his chest pumped with deep breaths.

"You're just like all the rest! I would have given you everything. Now you have to die."

Danielle balled her fists and struck at his face. He drew back one hand, slapped her and regained his hold on her neck. His fingers tightened, and she struggled to breathe. The room grew dark. She blinked in an attempt to remain conscious, but Nathan's face faded before her eyes.

Jack and Will had crept about halfway across the yard when an almost inhuman bellow erupted through the top of the bunker. A woman's scream followed the roar, and Jack sprinted forward.

Without thought for his own safety, he jumped into the hole and landed on a staircase. At the bottom he could see Nathan bending over a bed. Jack couldn't see her face, but he recognized the dress Danielle had worn the night before.

Leaping to the floor, he lunged forward and tackled Nathan. The impact sent Nathan sprawling, and Jack was on top of him by the time Nathan hit the floor. Jack pressed his gun to Nathan's head. "Give me an excuse to pull the trigger."

Will appeared at his side and grabbed Nathan's arms. Together they dragged him to the staircase and handcuffed him to the railing.

Jack whirled and dashed back to the bed where Danielle lay unconscious. "She has a weak pulse, and I don't think she's breathing."

Will headed toward the steps. "I can't get a phone signal in here. I'll go outside and call nine-one-one."

"Wait," Jack yelled. "Help me get her onto the floor."

Will ran back to Jack and grabbed Danielle's legs.

Jack took her shoulders, and they laid her on the floor. Jack leaned over her, tilted her head back and listened for breathing, but he heard nothing. "I'm going to start CPR. You go call for help."

Pinching her nose closed, Jack lowered his mouth to hers and blew two breaths into her mouth. "Come on, Danielle. Breathe."

Her chest didn't rise, and he laced his fingers together and placed them on her chest. He counted the compressions as he pumped. "One, two, three…"

When he counted thirty, he opened her mouth again and gave two short breaths. Still no movement.

From the staircase, Nathan chuckled. "You can't save her. She's dead."

Will hurried back down the stairs and stopped beside Jack as he began the next thirty compressions. "I got through to the department. They're on their way with an ambulance."

Jack nodded and kept pumping. He had completed ten when she coughed. Jack bent forward. "Danielle, can you hear me?"

The sight of her chest's rise and fall brought tears to his eyes. She took two deep breaths and opened her eyes. She blinked and stared up at him. She tried to speak, but he put his fingers on her lips.

"Don't move. Help is on the way. Just rest. I'm here with you, and I'm never going to let anything happen to you again."

She smiled and inched her hand toward his. "Jack," she whispered.

He grabbed her hand and brought her fingers to his lips. "I love you, Danielle. Everything is going to be all right."

She squeezed his hand, smiled and closed her eyes.

Will sat down on the bed and patted him on the back. "I'm glad your hunch paid off, Jack. If we hadn't been here, she'd be dead by now."

Jack glanced across at Nathan handcuffed to the stairs. He no longer looked like the domineering head of a university. His eyes twitched as his gaze appeared to bounce off the walls of the small room. A low babbling rose from his mouth. "Danielle should have listened to me. She's no different than the others."

Will jerked a finger in Nathan's direction. "He started saying that when you were doing CPR, and he keeps repeating it."

Jack looked back at Danielle who appeared to be sleeping. He wished he could make her more comfortable, but he was afraid to move her until the EMTs arrived. Right now he just wanted to look at her and thank God that her life had been spared.

The next day Danielle lay on the couch in her living room. Her father sat reading the newspaper in a chair beside her. Dishes rattled in the kitchen where her mother was preparing dinner.

Her father lowered the newspaper. His shoulder-length hair swayed as he shook his head and peered over the wire-rimmed glasses perched on the end of his nose. "The paper says that the police have charged Nathan Webster with three counts of murder here, and that he faces one count in Chapel Hill."

Danielle nodded. "Stan's death. He told me he killed Stan."

Her father folded the newspaper and laid it on the coffee table. "I can't believe that man was such a monster. I can never repay Jack for what he did for us. If anything had happened to you…" He bit his lip.

Danielle reached over and patted his hand. "I'm safe now, and the doctor says I should be able to go to Atlanta by the first of next week."

"Do you still want to go, baby girl?"

She sat up straight. "Of course I do."

"What about Jack?"

Her heart pricked, but she forced a smile to her face. "I've hardly seen Jack since my rescue."

He reached over and squeezed her hand. "He wouldn't leave your side until he was sure you were going to be all right. He's been very busy today, but he's called several times. Your mother and I really like him and wouldn't mind having him in the family."

She frowned at a memory, or maybe it was a dream. It seemed as if she remembered Jack saying he loved her. She shook her head. That was probably her subconscious wanting him to say those words.

Before she could answer her father, the doorbell rang, and he jumped up. "I'll get it." He hurried to the door and opened it. "Come in, Jack. It's good to see you."

Danielle swung her feet to the floor and sat up, but Jack rushed toward her. "Don't get up. You're still weak."

She laughed and sank back into the couch's cushions. "My parents have tried to make me an invalid, but I'm fine."

He smiled. "I'm glad."

Her father coughed and backed away. "I think I'll go help Mary with supper. You're staying, Jack. We won't take no for an answer."

Jack laughed. "Okay." He waited until her father had left the room before he sat down in the chair next to the couch. "I'll stay if you want me to, Danielle."

"I do. I've hardly seen you since I woke up in the hospital, so I'm glad to have an opportunity to thank you for saving my life."

"I was just doing my job."

She'd been so happy to see him when he came into the room, and now she felt deflated. "So it was just another case?"

His eyebrows arched. "I didn't mean that. Of course you're more to me than another case."

"How?"

He frowned. "What do you mean how?"

She leaned forward and propped her hands on her hips. "When Nathan was choking the life out of me, the only thing I could think of was that I wouldn't see you again. Then I opened my eyes, and you were there. Now you come here, and I see the Jack that I first met, all reserved and afraid to show his feelings."

He swallowed, rose to his feet and began to pace back and forth. "I had my speech prepared today. I knew exactly what I was going to say. Then I come in here and see you lying on that couch, and I remember how scared I was when I was pumping your chest trying to get you to breathe. I didn't think I could live if anything happened to you. That's why I kept praying that God would save you so I could tell you how much I love you."

She pushed to her feet, grabbed his arm and stopped him midstride. "What did you say?"

He stared into her eyes. "I said I love you."

She shook her head. "No, not that. The part about God."

He smiled. "You were right, Danielle. I finally came up against something I couldn't handle alone, and God was right there waiting to help me through it. If you hadn't kept after me about turning to God, I might never have known the peace that I have now." He wrapped his arms around her and drew her close. "So you really saved my life before I saved yours."

She circled her arms around his neck. "So you've made peace with the past?"

"Yes, and I want a future with you. I love you, Danielle. Marry me."

"I love you, too, Jack." A thought struck her, and she pulled away from him. "What about your work? I can't live in Webster Falls anymore."

He laughed and pulled her back to him. "I can't, either. I'm thinking about moving to Atlanta. I've been offered this good job with an organization that's starting a mission to the Batwa people in Africa. It seems the rock star who runs the project needs someone to oversee security, and he thinks I'd be perfect."

She squealed and hugged him. "You're going to work with us?"

His eyes bored into her. "I am. God just keeps surprising me with blessings. He's given me the most wonderful woman in the world and a job with my teenage rock idols." His lips trembled. "Your father is a good man, Danielle. He's made arrangements for my mother to be placed in a facility in Atlanta that deals with her condition, and he insists on paying for her care because I saved your life."

She stared up at him. "I can't believe it."

"What?"

"When I first met you, I thought you were a remote, private person who detested being a member of the human race. Now you're going to help minister to people in Africa. God sure can work miracles."

He smiled. "I've got a lot to learn, but with your help I'll make it."

Once she'd thought his eyes cold and aloof. Now she could see only love in their depths. "We'll make it together."

His lips moved closer. "I didn't know I could ever be this happy. Thank you, Danielle, for saving me from myself."

* * * * *

Dear Reader,

I hope you enjoyed reading *Mountain Peril*. As I wrote this book, the story and the characters became very special to me. At times Jack and Danielle became so real in my mind that I had trouble remembering they were products of my imagination.

I grieved for Danielle's losses, and I sympathized with Jack for the troubles he'd endured since childhood. In the end, though, what they needed was what we all desire—the assurance that God loves us and is concerned about every aspect of our lives.

Years from now this story may be a dim memory for you. However, I hope the truth that I've tried to convey will always be in your heart. The Psalmist said it best when he wrote: *You are forgiving and good, O Lord, abounding in love to all who call to You.* Psalm 86:5.

Sandra Robbins

QUESTIONS FOR DISCUSSION

1. Danielle lived for years with the unsolved murder of her best friend and then her fiancé. Have you had to cope with such a tragedy in your life? If so, how did it affect you?

2. Jack felt as an adult he had become like his unloving father. How do you think childhood experiences shape the adults we become?

3. Danielle's parents had faced the demons of drug abuse and with God's help had conquered their addictions. How can we as Christians help those we see struggling to overcome habits that are ruining their lives?

4. Danielle feared loving someone because she couldn't face the possibility that she might lose them. How do we overcome such fears?

5. Jack felt responsible for his wife's death because he thought he drove her into the arms of another man. Do you think his actions played a part in her death, or do you think she was responsible for her choices?

6. When you make a mistake in life, do you tend to blame someone else, or do you take responsibility for your actions?

7. Jack's inner thoughts reveal a very sensitive man who guards his emotions. Do you know someone like that? How do you reach that person to let them know you care about what troubles them?

8. Danielle had been taught by her parents to love all people, regardless of race or socioeconomic status, but her superiors at the university didn't share her beliefs. How do you deal with people who demonstrate attitudes contrary to what Jesus taught?

9. Danielle told Jack that he would one day face something that he couldn't handle alone. Do you try to solve your problems by yourself, or do you rely on the strength of the Lord and His guidance to help you through troubling times?

10. Since his mother's diagnosis with Alzheimer's, Jack had felt alone and missed the woman who didn't recognize him. Does your family struggle with a debilitating disease? How do you cope?

11. Danielle is surprised that Jack is joining their ministry to the Batwa people of Africa. Have

you ever been involved in a mission trip that ministered to destitute people either in this country or abroad? How did it affect your life?

12. Jack comes to see the need for having God in his life and prays for forgiveness for denying Him for so many years. Have you done the same in your life?

Here's a sneak peek at
THE WEDDING GARDEN
by Linda Goodnight,
the second book in her new miniseries
REDEMPTION RIVER,
available in May 2010 from Love Inspired.

One step into the living room and she froze again, pan aloft.

A hulking shape stood in shadow just inside the French doors leading out to the garden veranda. This was not Popbottle Jones. This was a big, bulky, dangerous-looking man. She raised the pan higher.

"What do you want?"

"Annie?" He stepped into the light.

All the blood drained from Annie's face. Her mouth went dry as saltines. "Sloan Hawkins?"

The man removed a pair of silver aviator sunglasses and hung them on the neck of his black rock-and-roll T-shirt. He'd rolled the sleeves up, baring muscular biceps. A pair of eyes too blue to define narrowed, looking her over as though he were a wolf and she a bunny rabbit.

Annie suppressed an annoying shiver.

It was Sloan, all right, though older and with more muscle. His nearly black hair was shorter now—no more bad-boy curl over the forehead—but bad boy screamed off him in waves just the same. He was devastatingly handsome, in a tough, rugged, manly kind of way. The years had been kind to Sloan Hawkins.

She really wanted to hate him, but she'd already wasted too much emotion on this outlaw. With God's help she'd learned to forgive. But she wasn't about to forget.

Will Sloan and Annie's faith be strong
enough to see them through
the pain of the past and allow them to open
their hearts to a possible future?
Find out in THE WEDDING GARDEN
by Linda Goodnight,
available May 2010 from Love Inspired.

HEARTWARMING INSPIRATIONAL ROMANCE

Contemporary,
inspirational romances
with Christian characters
facing the challenges
of life and love
in today's world.

**NOW AVAILABLE IN REGULAR
AND LARGER-PRINT FORMATS.**

**Steeple
Hill®**

For exciting stories that reflect traditional values,
visit:

www.SteepleHill.com

Love Inspired. HISTORICAL

INSPIRATIONAL HISTORICAL ROMANCE

Engaging stories of romance,
adventure and faith,
these novels are set in
various historical periods
from biblical times
to World War II.

NOW AVAILABLE!

Steeple Hill®